Things That Go Bump in a Canadian Night

Ronald Wolf

<Ronald Wolf>
<2014>

Copyright © <2014> by <Ronald Wolf>

All rights reserved. This book or any portion thereof may not be reproduced or used in any manner whatsoever without the express written permission of the publisher except for the use of brief quotations in a book review or scholarly journal.

First Printing: <2014>

ISBN <978-1-312-10713-7>

Dedication

I wish to thank Gary Erb. Without his proofreading skills, this book would have many errors.

I wish to thank Pauline Hyatt. She spent countless hours on helping me formatt this book and advised me that this would make a great book.

No words can effectively thank these people. Thank you. Without your support and patience, I would never have achieved my dream.

Preface

Things That Go Bump in a Canadian Night is my first book which covers the paranormal in Canada.

This book is meant to be light hearted, interesting and above all, fun to read.

Is there life after death, is there life other than us in the universe? I don't have the answers.

What I can tell you is that I took the time to interview the people in this book in a professional manner.

This book is a collection of stories I wrote a few years back. They were printed in a weekly column entitled Things That Go Bump in a Canadian Night.

I hope you like this book and feel free to contact me at rwolf65@hotmail.com

Ronald Wolf

CHAMP

You ever wonder what's in our water we drink? It depends on where you live. You could be drinking water from a well, purified water or lake water. If you're drinking lake water then fish swim in the water you drink as well as many other plankton-sized crustations.

If you live near the waters of Lake Champlain there may be other creatures, not so microscopic, that share your water. The world calls this creature Champ

But who is Champ? One theory suggests that Champ is a dinosaur that managed to escape extinction and lives on in Lake Champlain. Another suggests that the creatures could be surviving zeuglodons, a primitive form of whale with a long snake like body.

These creatures have been thought to be long extinct, however fossils of them have been found a few miles from Lake Champlain in Charlotte, Vt. Champ might also be a Lake Sturgeon.

There are sturgeons in Lake Champlain and they can grow to great lengths. They are a very old, almost prehistoric fish with a scaleless body that is supported by a partially cartilaginous skeleton along with rows of scales.

Its single dorsal fin, running along its spine, would match many descriptions of Champ, although its sharp, shark-like tail would not.

Another theory is that Champ could be related to a plesiosaur. A plesiosaur is a prehistoric water dwelling reptile (not a dinosaur) with a long snake-like head and four large flippers. Plesiosaurs loved fish and other aquatic animals.

Scientists date the plesiosaur to the Triassic period, 200 million years ago, through the Cretaceous period, about 65 million years ago (when all dinosaurs are thought to have gone extinct).

For almost 400 years, sighting of Champ has been seen by many. Here are a few reported sightings of the legendary creature.

There have been at least 300 reported unexplained sightings of Champ over the years.

There is no certainty when the first sighting of Champ was; however, the creature was depicted by Native Americans. It was said that Samuel de Champlain saw Champ in 1609.

This claim that he spotted a strange monster has been traced by historians to actually have occurred in the St. Lawrence estuary however.

Other sightings include: 1819: Bulwagga Bay, Port Henry, NY; 1871: Horseshoe Bay, riders of the steamship Curlew claimed to see a head and long neck that created quite a wake.; 1870: Charlotte, Vt., a full steamboat spotted Champ; 1873: Dresden, NY., another steamboat full spotted Champ; 1945: In the middle of the lake the creature was spotted by the famous S.S. Ticonderoga; 1954: A 14 inch reptile was trapped in Shelburne Bay, possibly a baby; 1977: The Mansi photograph was taken by Sandra Mansi, a tourist from Connecticut, with her Kodak Instamatic, of what she called a dinosaur. This has become the most famous piece of evidence featured nationally in Time Magazine and the New York Times among others; 1984: Off Appletree Point, Vt. 86 passengers aboard the Ethan Allen spotted three to five humps which disappeared after about three minutes due to the approach of a speed boat; 1993: Button Bay State Park, Ferrisburgh, Vt. A baby Champ reportedly swam between two women bathers; 1995: Dennis Hall of Champ Quest recorded Champ on video.

Champ is serving as a mascot for Lake Champlain Land Trust. In the eyes of the Lake Champlain Land Trust, Champ embodies the mysteries, wonders and importance of the lake and the creatures that may or may not live within.

The fact that we do not know whether Champ exists, means there is still an undiscovered and protected portion of the lake left to discover.

Perhaps most importantly, Champ helps educate the public about this beautiful place and gives us all a reason to sit quietly by the lake and ponder what lies beneath.

Whether they live in the woods, above or beneath the earth or in the waters of Canada, legendary creatures may not be proven but they all have a place in Things That Go Bump In a Canadian Night and it's getting more crowded by the week.

CANADIAN UFOs

Astronauts planted the seeds for humanity. These astronauts could be called Unidentified Flying Objects or UFOs.

Some theorists believe that there's been an alien UFO presence on Earth since the earliest days of civilization and the evidence of this presence can be found in ancient art.

Peculiar figures and flying objects can be found in ancient art dating back to the earliest cave drawings. In France, the cave of "Pech Merle" near "Le Cabrerets" is host to cave drawings which date back to from 17000 to 15000 BC.

The list is as endless as the stars in the heavens. In virtually every civilization there are two things in common: religion and paintings or drawings that tells a story of people or creatures and their ships from other planets. In modern day Canada there are many sightings of UFOs.

Dave Francis and Kelly McDonald witnessed a UFO over University College of the Frasier Valley campus in Chilliwack, B.C., and Francis said, "I really think it was a UFO. I don't really care if anybody else believes me...it was the craziest thing I ever saw."

Whatever it was, they were moving from place to place as a unit [and then] just faded away." McDonald said.

"I know that I saw something that wasn't from here. I've never seen anything move that way. It wasn't birds. [As the UFO approached] it broke apart into 20 or more of these little spheres ... birds don't dive-bomb in at each other."

During the night of January 25, 2010, witnesses in Harbour Mille, N.L., reported multiple UFO sightings. A photograph taken by a resident revealed one of the UFOs to resemble a missile. An investigation by the community's police force and the RCMP is under way, though the Office of the Prime Minister has stated that the UFOs were not missiles.

Another minor report of this incident came from Calgary where boys playing hockey reported seeing similar objects where they stated

"We thought they were transformers."

The following were observed in the province of Manitoba.

In February 1975, north of Lundar a farmer walking to his barn saw a basketball-sized light swooping over him. As he gazed up, he felt as if hot plastic was poured over his face.

On March 27, 1975, near Graysville, at 2 a.m., a young girl wakes up to a shrill siren-like pulsating sound, and an earthquake-like tremble. She saw a red ball of light, as bright as the sun, zipping southwards.

On April 10, 1975, near Carman a Diemert couple was walking to their private airfield, when they saw a large red slow-moving light, hovering at the tree line. They saw a disk-shaped object with a dome attached. It then turned direction and disappeared after five minutes.

April 3, 1976, near Sperling around 8 p.m., an orange ball of light was observed to suddenly appear over a bridge, about five feet (1.5 m) wide. As the observers followed in a car, they saw a second ball appear over their car. The objects reportedly disappeared or receded when they were chased, but then suddenly reappeared when they started leaving.

Many people now believe in UFOs or at the very least, we are not alone in this or any other universes. To think that we are the only ones existing is ludicrous.

If there is intelligent life capable of space travel, would they visit earth? What can we offer these travelers or can these travelers offer us something of value? Perhaps they can offer us the recipe for everlasting peace on our own planet.

THE LOUP-GAROU

A werewolf is one of the oldest legends you can sink your teeth into. For hundreds of years the werewolf has been frightening and enchanting readers by candlelight and recently, viewers on the silver screen.

The word werewolf comes from various languages. In almost every language, werewolf has their own particular meanings.

Loup-Garou, the werewolf, is known but less widespread in French Canadian folklore than in Europe. The Loup-Garou is not always a wolf or dog, but may also take the form of a calf or small ox, a pig, a cat or even an owl.

The spell could last for as long as 101 days, taking hold of the victim every evening, which then forced to wander the countryside in animal form. The spell might be broken if someone recognized the individual while transformed and could draw blood from the animal; neither person could speak of this incident, for fear of worse reprisals.

The legend was often used to scare children into behaving. "Make yo' bed or da loupgarou is gonna get ya'!" What makes these creatures so dangerous is the fact that while in their wolf form, they are completely aware and as intelligent as they are in their human form.

With their enhanced abilities and senses, it makes them difficult to be destroyed. Along with these abilities, they differ from the werewolf because it isn't just the moon that can change them. These creatures can change at their own will, as well as by the command of a full moon. These are magnificent creatures...but beware of the Loup Garou.

Werewolves are often attributed super-human strength and senses, far beyond those of both wolves and men. Though it is endowed with all the beastly implements like stout-jaws and offensive paws that a natural wolf is most likely to use during a conflict with its enemy or prey, it has been classically known to kill the others with a dagger or a knife though bite marks are also found on the (generally) dead victim.

The werewolf is generally held as a European character, although its lore spread through the world in later times. Shape-shifters, similar to werewolves, are common in tales from all over the world, most notably amongst the Native Americans, though most of them involve animal forms other than wolves.

Werewolves are a frequent subject of modern fictional books, although fictional werewolves have been attributed traits distinct from those of original folklore, most notably vulnerability to silver bullets. Werewolves continue to endure in modern culture and fiction, with books, films and television shows cementing the werewolf's stance as a dominant figure in horror.

Many European countries and cultures influenced by them have stories of werewolves, including: Albania, Armenia, Croatia/Bosnia France, Greece, Spain, Argentina, Mexico, Bulgaria-Turkey, (CzechRepulic/Slovakia, Serbia/Mont enegro, Belarus, Russia, Ukraine, Poand,Romania,Macedonia,Slovenia, Scotland,England,Ireland,Wales,Germany, the Netherlands,Denmark, Sweden, Norway, Iceland,

Galicia Brazil, Lithuania, Latvia, Andorra, Catalonia, Hungary,

Estonia,Finland, Italy.

In rare occasions, people believe that they can become, in reality, werewolves.

Clinical lycanthropy is defined as a rare psychiatric syndrome that a person can or has transformed into an animal or that he or she is an animal. Its name is connected to the mythical condition of lycanthropy, a supernatural affliction in which people are said to physically shape shift into wolves. The terms zoanthropy and therianthropy are also sometimes used for the delusion that one has turned into an animal in general and not specifically a wolf.

In folklore or in reality the werewolf is definitely an old, if not ancient part of mankind and a recent submission in Things That Go Bump In a Canadian Night.

FORT ERIE

Like most Canadian forts, Fort Erie is rich in Canadian history, war and of course, spirits of soldiers who defended the fort with their very lives. Today, we pay homage to Fort Erie and their soldiers, who fought and died, for their homeland. The War of 1812 was a significant period of Canadian history for the fort.

Fort Erie was unfinished when the United States declared war on June 18, 1812. Fort Erie was held for a period by U.S. forces and then abandoned on June 9, 1813. The fort also played a huge part of The Underground Railroad in the mid 1850s when American slaves found freedom in Canada.

Daryl Learn, senior interpreter for the fort, has been holding his title for six years. He has heard and seen some strange, weird and even paranormal events.

Most paranormal events have centered on war time. For example, people have seen foot prints in the snow from the inner gate to where the outer gate used to stand.

The foot prints were flat sole horseshoe heel very much like the hobnail style.

People often heard a voice calling out to them in the dark, challenging them as a guard would.

"We actually believe it was a man who froze to death in 1810. In that year guards were on duty for 30 minutes at a time but when they came to relieve him, he already froze to death. He was leaning on the gate when they found him."

The guard is only seen when it is snowing or in the winter Learn said. "In our upper museum people hear a small girl crying and calling for her mother."

Young women in their early 20s and pregnant women are the ones who often hear the young girl but some men would hear the cries as well.

"One former staff member still won't go up there." In the officer quarters Captain Kinsley served in the Kings Aid Regiment was believed to have died in his bed from. The Ug which is a mix of some basic lung diseases.

"He actually drowned in his sleep in his bed. We had reports up there from very simple things from people hearing whispering, feet shuffling on the floor, people hearing shrieks coming from the room, stomping up and down the stairs, windows and doors opening and closing."

During our All-Hallows-Eve tour we always have the newest employee to stay in the fort in case a visitor would wander off somewhere by mistake.

We would have a burning of Guy Fox outside near the fort, he said.

It was six years this October that

an event took place. That year since it was Learn's first year he was the one who acted as guard in the fort.

In the parade square an event happened to the new employee.

"I'll swear by it that a man came out of the kitchen. He was a tall guy he looked like he was wearing a top hat or something like that. I thought it was just a visitor. I thought he was someone to get more cookies for sale.

"I called down to get his attention and direct him back up to the burning of Guy Fox. He paused, turned; I couldn't make out a single feature of the guy other than his eyes. They were pure white. That scared the ever living daylights out of me. Every bone in my body said to run away but part of me said it was a joke."

The figure made its way to the gun powder magazine Learn ran after him expecting to see one of the employees playing a joke on him.

"But there was nobody down there and the door to the kitchen was locked."

There are many other paranormal activities the fort holds. Should you be in the area of Fort Erie, On., be part of the Friday night tour if you dare.

NANABOZHO & THE SPIRIT BRIDE

Nanabozho is the Ojibwetrickster figure and culture hero. He plays a similar role as the Saulteaux Wiisagejaak (Cree Wisakedjak). The Algonquin had a similar figure called Ganoozhigaabe (AbenakiGluskabe).

Nanabozho was one of four sons of Wiininwaa ("Nourishment") a human mother, and E-bangishimog ("In the West"), a spirit father.

Nanabozho most often appears in the shape of a rabbit and is characterized as a trickster. In his rabbit form, he is called Mishaabooz ("Great rabbit" or "Hare") or Chi-waabooz ("Big rabbit"). He was sent to Earth by Gitchi Manitou to teach the Ojibwe. One of his first tasks was to name all the plants and animals. Nanabozho is considered to be the founder of Midewiwin. Like the Egyptian god Thoth, he is thought to be the inventor of fishing and hieroglyphs. He is a shape-shifter and a cocreator of the world.

In more recent myths among the Ojibwe, Nanabozho saves the forests from Paul Bunyan. They fought for forty days and nights, and Nanabozho killed Bunyan with a Red Lake walleye.

There was once a young warrior whose bride died on the eve of their wedding. Although he had distinguished himself by his bravery and goodness, the death left the young man devastated.

He was unable to eat or sleep. Instead of hunting with the others, he just spent time at the grave of his bride, staring into the air.

However, one day he happened to overhear some elders speaking about the path to the spirit world. He listened intently and memorized the directions to the minutest detail. He had heard that the spirit world was far to the south. He immediately set out on his journey. After two weeks, he still saw no change in the landscape to indicate that the spirit world was near.

Then he emerged from the forest and saw the most beautiful plane he had ever seen. In the distance was a small hut where an ancient wise man lived. He asked the wise man for directions.

The old man knew exactly who the warrior was and whom he sought. He told the lad that the bride had passed by only a day before. In order to follow her, the warrior would have to leave his body behind and press on in his spirit.

The spirit world itself is an island in a large lake that can be reached only by canoes waiting on this shore. However, the old man warned him not to speak to his bride until they were both safely on the island of the spirits.

Soon the old man recited some magic chants and the warrior felt his spirit leave his body. Now a spirit, he walked along the shore and saw a birch bark canoe. Not a stone's throw away was his bride, entering her own canoe. As he made his way across the water and looked at her, he saw that she duplicated his every stroke. Why didn't they travel together? One can only enter the spirit world alone and be judged only on one's individual merits.

Midway through the journey, a tempest arose. It was more terrible than any he had ever seen. Some of the spirits in canoes were swept away by the storm - these were those who had been evil in life. Since both the warrior and his bride were good, they made it through the tempest without incident and soon the water was as smooth as glass beneath a cloudless sky.

The island of the blessed was a beautiful place where it was always late spring, with blooming flowers and cloudless skies, never too warm or too cold. He met his bride on the shore and took her hand. They had not walked ten steps together when a soft sweet voice spoke to them; it was the Master of Life.

The Master told them that the young warrior must return as he came; it wasn't his time yet. He was to carefully trace his steps back to his body, put it on, and return home. He did this and became a great chief, happy in the assurance that he would see his bride once again.

Some legends, folklore, myths and even haunting, bump louder and harder than others but they all bump in a Canadian night.

HAUNTED CANADIAN CEMETERIES

What can be said about graveyards or cemeteries? As far as horror movies are concerned they are places where the dead come to life and attack the living. Some people claim they are places of peace and rest.

Ross Bay Cemetery, Victoria, B.C.

This is the final resting place for many famous people of Victoria and the scene of several ghosts. The spirit of Isabella Ross can be seen, usually looking out over the water. She owned the land where the cemetery was built. There is also the sighting of an unknown lady dressed in white.

The misty clad apparition of David Fee is spotted from time to time. He was murdered outside of St. Andrew's Cathedral in 1890 on Christmas Eve. The ghosts of a couple dressed in Victorian clothing have been seen floating around the west side of the cemetery. Visitors have sometimes spotted a lady darting around in a panic looking for her lost child.

Drummond Hill Cemetery, Niagara Falls, On.

This is one of the world's most famous haunted cemeteries. It is a cemetery I have visited. During the day, the place is peaceful and full of history. At night, well, at night that is a different story. I didn't venture too far passed the iron gates. I consider myself to be extremely brave or fool hardy. I don't know which but I felt something or someone waiting for me in the dark.

The cemetery itself boasts numerous historical aspects. It holds the graves of both British and American soldiers, who lost their lives in the Battle of Lundy's Lane on July, 1814. It's also the resting place for Laura Secord, one of Canada's heroines recognized for her contribution in the War of 1812. Be sure to visit the sculpture of Laura

Secord, with the creepy eyes that seem to follow you wherever you move!

Although this in itself is quite freaky, keep in mind it's just an artistic device used by the sculptor. There are also many important archaeological resources to be found in the area because of the many military artifacts buried there from the war.

To this day, Drummond Hill Cemetery is said to be one of the most haunted cemeteries in all of Canada. Spirits tend to haunt the place they called home, a place they loved, or the place where they tragically died. Many lives were lost on this very same land, making it a hotbed full of ghostly activity.

It is said that apparition of five old soldiers, dressed as Royal Scots, can be seen limping across the battlefield, only to disappear far away in the distance. The apparition of three British soldiers have also been seen trudging up the hill, then marching, as if they are still going about their duties.

SKELETON PARK MCBURNEY PARK
Kingston, On.

Back in 1813 to 1865 this park was known as Kingston's Upper Cemetery. What this was, was a mass cemetery/grave site containing more than 100,000 bodies which all died from contagious epidemics.

In 1894, the municipal government tried to remove the remains but many locals objected due to fear that contagious diseases might start again if dug up. The cemetery was transformed into Frontenac Park in 1895 and then became what it is known as today Mc Burney Park in 1965. It is said that over the years many different remains have surfaced throughout the park giving it the nickname Skeleton Park.

Do ghosts haunt cemeteries? I don't know. If I was a ghost I personally wouldn't. I would be among the friends I have left behind. I would play practical jokes on people and perhaps have a spirit or two with those that bump in a Canadian night.

BLYTHEWOOD MANOR BED & BREAKFAST

Any paranormal researcher knows that the region of Niagara Falls, On. is a hot spot for those that bump in a Canadian night.

When Stef (Stefanie) and I first found the place (the building) we fell in love with it. We had a short tour of the inside and came back later to have a proper tour with the real estate agent. It was at that time we both sensed a female sprit at the top of the stairs and later we both agreed that she felt sad, recalled Wayne Mallows, owner.

"When we moved in, things seemed to be a lot more peaceful than when we first began looking at the place."

Mallows said he had spoken with a friend who had a long time friend who was a medium and she in turn had contacted me about the house.

She told me many things about the previous owners and also told me the spirit woman was very pleased with me, that I had good manners. She went on to tell me that there was a hidden treasure in the house but then cautioned me that it may only be a child's toy that had been lost but had been valuable to him or her, said Mallows.

"When I was working on the garage one afternoon I thought to myself, 'I wonder what the treasure is?' I was up on a ladder and at that moment, I heard a woman's voice say in my right ear; "the house is the treasure."

"It was so real I actually turned to see who it was that had spoke to me and realized I was up 15 feet and quite alone."

I saw the figure of a woman walk through the kitchen from when the old servant's stairs used to be, (they're still there but closed off) and move towards what was once the kitchen pantry. She was solid and dark in colour. She had what appeared to me as having her hair up. I could only see her upper body as the kitchen table and chairs blocked her lower half from my view. I saw her while I was sitting in the living room which opens onto the dining room and a short hallway joins the dining room to the kitchen, noted Mallows.

The Mallows would often smell cigar smoke on the veranda and in the living room, which was originally the gentleman's smoking room.

Stef would often smell a rose-like fragrance on the first floor on numerous occasions. We do not use any rose scented cleaners or air fresheners, added Mallows.

"One night Stef thought my son, Stephen, was coming into the kitchen from the dining room. So real was this image that she said hello to him then carried on talking to me. After a moment she looked into the hallway to see why he had not come into the kitchen, there was no one there.

"The door that leads to the kitchen from the dining room makes a very distinctive noise when it's opened or closed over. Many a night while in bed we hear that door open and close again," finished Mallows.

Some spirits might become angered when new people move into their abode. In this case, it is the reverse. The spirit of a woman seems to become less stressed if spirits do have human emotions.

THE WENDIGO

You probably won't find a more savage or terrifying creature as the Wendigo. Americans and Canadians share this legend which is very similar to a werewolf. The Wendigo (also known as Windigo, Weendigo, Windago, Windiga, Witiko, Wihtikow), is a mythical creature appearing in the mythology of the Algonquian people.

It is a malevolent cannibalistic spirit which humans could transform, or which could possess humans. Those who indulged in cannibalism were at particular risk, and the legend appears to have reinforced this practice as taboo.

Wendigo psychosis is a culture-bound disorder which involves an intense craving for human flesh and the fear that one will turn into a cannibal. This once occurred frequently among Algonquian Native cultures, though has declined with the Native American urbanization.

Recently, the Wendigo has also become a horror entity of contemporary literature and film, much like the vampire, werewolf, or zombie, although these fictional depictions often bear little resemblance to the original entity.

The Wendigo is part of the traditional belief systems of various Algonquian-speaking tribes in the northern United States and Canada, most notably the Ojibwa/Saulteaux, the Cree, and the Inu/Naskapi/Montagnais.

Though descriptions varied somewhat, common to all these cultures was the conception of Wendigos as malevolent, cannibalistic, supernatural beings (manitous) of great spiritual power.

They were strongly associated with the winter, the North, and coldness, as well as with famine and starvation. At the same time, Wendigos were embodiments of gluttony, greed, and excess; never satisfied after killing and consuming one person, they were constantly searching for new victims.

In some traditions, humans who became overpowered by greed could turn into Wendigos; the Wendigo myth thus served as a method of encouraging cooperation and moderation. Among the Ojibwa, Eastern Cree, Westmain Swampy Cree, and Innu/Naskapi/Montagnais, Wendigos were said to be giants, many times larger than human beings (a characteristic absent from the Wendigo myth in the other Algonquian cultures).

Whenever a Wendigo ate another person, it would grow larger, in proportion to the meal it had just eaten, so that it could never be full. Wendigos were therefore simultaneously constantly gorging themselves and emaciated from starvation.

All cultures in which the Wendigo myth appeared shared the belief that human beings could turn into Wendigos if they ever resorted to cannibalism or, alternately, become possessed by the demonic spirit of a Wendigo, often in a dream.

Once transformed, a person would become violent and obsessed with eating human flesh. The most frequent cause of transformation into a Wendigo was if a person had resorted to cannibalism, consuming the body of another human in order to keep from starving to death during a time of extreme hardship or famine.

Among northern Algonquian cultures, cannibalism, even to save one's own life, was viewed as a serious taboo; the proper response to famine was suicide or resignation to death. On one level, the Wendigo myth thus worked as a deterrent and a warning against resorting to cannibalism; those who did would become Wendigo monsters themselves.

Among the Assiniboine, the Cree and the Ojibwa, a satirical ceremonial dance was originally performed during times of famine to reinforce the seriousness of the Wendigo taboo.

The ceremonial dance, known as a wiindigookaanzhimowin in Ojibwe and today performed as part of the last day activities of the Sun dance, involves wearing a mask and dancing about the drum backwards. The last known Wendigo Ceremony conducted in the United States was at Lake Windigo of Star Island of Cass Lake, located within the Leech Lake Indian Reservation in northern Minnesota.

The Wendigo creature is now part of the things that go bump in a Canadian night.

THE LEGEND OF CAPTAIN BLACK BARTELMY

Captain Black Bartelmy wasn't the kind of person that would win father of the year award or be hailed as a good fellow. Not in the least. You see, he was a pirate. As a nasty pirate who not only killed his wife but also his children.

It was in the Atlantic Coast that he inflicted his evil deeds along with the worst dredges of the universe. The countryside was also played victim to his grizzly deeds too terrible to mention here.

Before he landed in Cape Forchu, N.S., Bartelmy and his ship was loaded with so much treasure, 500 treasure chests, that it was told that his ship appeared that it could sink at that time, laying his booty to the dark waters below. Suddenly, a fog, as thick as pea soup, rolled in to the bay.

A tide soon took hold of his ship at Roaring Bull and started to smash the ship to pieces. But before all on board was killed Bartelmy spotted land and with the aid of his trusted mate Ben the Hook and the rest of the crew took as much booty as the escape boat could hold.

What was the reward for the crew that helped with the riches? Some would say it could be a percentage of the booty. The truth was hideous. Under the orders of Bartelmy, Ben slit the necks of the crew and tossed their bodies into the deadly sea.

Ben and Bartelmy climbed into the overloaded boat and rowed, like demons from hell, to calmer waters in the cape. Almost immediately the men looked for a safe place to hide their murderous booty. A large cave soon became visible and the men stock piled the treasure into the belly of the cave.

The men piled heavy rocks in the entrance of the cave and it was here that Ben received his just deserts. Bartelmy thrusted a sword into his mate's chest. The last sight and sounds of Ben were that of Bartelmy's laughing face. Now, tell me, was anyone really surprised by Bartelmy's actions?

Bartelmy was all alone with no one to talk to or kill. Soon hunger set in. No fast food places or coffee shops could be found anywhere. The evil Bartelmy's tummy started to growl. He got the idea that he should seek out a town or some food to eat. So, off he went in search of some grub. After walking along the shore line he soon found the land rising.

Bartelmy found himself in the sand of death-quicksand.

Bartelmy's last curse words were in a form of curses which was all in vain for only the seagulls, some of which defecated on the evil pirate's head, could hear the curses.

The local lighthouse keeper swore that he could see a flare shooting into the air soon after Bartelmy's death. The keeper thought a ship was in trouble and soon a rescue team was set forth to the sight of the flare.

As the rescue team neared the distressed vessel they were greeted by no other than Bartelmy himself or at the very least, Bartelmy's ghost! Bartelmy was seen waving a cutlass sword into the air laughing like a demon from hell. If you plan to visit the cape or the Roaring Bull take heed that you don't find yourself a victim of Bartelmy.

THE SLEEPING GIANT

Canada is a great land with room enough for all people from all walks of life. There is a time to grow as a country and a time to celebrate our diversities. This is the time to read legends from our ancestors of Canada.

On an island just outside Thunder Bay, On., now known as Isle Royale, once lived a great tribe of Ojibway Natives.

Because of their loyalty to their Gods, and their peaceful and industrious mode of living, Nanabijou, the Spirit of the Deep Sea Water, decided to reward them.

One day he called their Chief to his great Thunder Temple on the mountain and warned him that if he told the secret to the white man, that he, Nanabijou would be turned to stone and the Ojibwa tribe perish.

The Chief gave his promise, and Nanabijou told him of the rich silver mine, now known as "Silver Islet". The Great Spirit told him to go to the highest point on Thunder Cape, and here he would find the entrance to a tunnel that would lead him to the centre of the mine. Apparently the Chief and his people found the mine, for the Ojibway became famous for their beautiful silver ornaments.

However, torture and even death failed to make the gallant Ojibwa divulge their secret and the Sioux chieftains had to devise another scheme to find the source of the Ojibway silver.

One day they summoned the most cunning scout to a pow-wow and a plan was formed.

The scout was to enter the Ojibway camp disguised as one of them.

He did this and in a few days succeeded in learning the secret of the island of silver.

Going to the mine at night he took several large pieces of the precious metal in order to prove to his chieftain that he had fulfilled his mission.

The scout however never returned to his camp, for on his way back he stopped at a white traders post to purchase some food. Having no furs or money with which to pay for the goods, he used a piece of the silver. Upon seeing such a large piece of the gleaming metal, two white men sought to obtain the whereabouts of its source, in order to make themselves fabulously rich.

After filling the Sioux scout with liquor they persuaded him to show them the way to the mine. When almost in sight of "Silver Islet" a terrific storm broke over the Cape.

The white men were drowned and the Native was found in a crazed condition floating aimlessly in his canoe, but the most extraordinary thing that had happened during the storm, was that where once a wide opening to the bay was, now lay what appeared to be a great sleeping figure of a man.

The Great Spirit's warning had been fulfilled and he had been turned to stone.

On a little island at the foot of the Sleeping Giant, can still be seen the partly submerged shafts of what was once the richest silver mine in the northwest.

White men have tried again and again to pump out the water that keeps flooding it from Lake Superior but without success.

Is it still under the curse of Nanabijou, Spirit of the Deep Sea Water...perhaps...who can tell?

There are numerous versions of the Legend of the Sleeping Giant and one is not necessarily more valid than another.

BROCKAMOUR MANOUR
Niagara-On-The-Lake, On.

You would be hard pressed to find a place richer in pre-Canadian history. This edition into paranormal Canada involved the War of 1812 and the Brockamour Manor. The following information was gathered from the website.

On June 18, 1812, the United States declared war on Britain and committed itself to take over the lands of Canada – a colony of Britain, which according to Thomas Jefferson, could be done by a "mere matter of marching."

Brock seared his legend into the hearts of Canadians during the War of 1812. First, with his bold and confident strategy at Detroit where, against all odds, he convinced General Hull to surrender, thus recapturing the Upper Canada lands lost without firing a shot.

During the early hours of October 13, 1812 Brock awoke to the sounds of cannon fire as the Americans again invaded Upper Canada at Queenston Heights. Jumping onto his horse he raced toward the battle, stopping only at the home of his love to say a brief good-bye.

It was the last time she saw him alive. While rallying his men, who were in disarray upon his arrival on the battle scene and leading them in a counter attack, he was easily identifiable in his red coat. A skilled American marksman stepped forward, shot and thus ended the life of Sir Isaac Brock.

Sophia stayed true to his memory living with her sister Isabella, who also became widowed, in the Powell house where Brock and she had met. It is this circumstance that gives this home its name, Brockamour signifying the love of Brock.

Owners Rick Jorgensen and Colleen Cone now own the historic Brockamour Country Inn for the past four years.

Jorgensen recounts some of the most intriguing events at the Inn since owning it.

A guest came down one day "freaked out" because his computer was turned off when he was working on it and the computer was playing music. He was in the room that people were commonly experiencing paranormal activity, he stated. He said that when he first moved in, the incidents happened frequently. Experiences did slow down in the last year however.

"The door bell would go off in the middle of the night. When I came down, there would be nobody here. It would happen exactly at the same time three or four times a week."

Two years ago a group of five women came to the Inn to try and experience the paranormal activity which surrounds the place.

"They showed us pictures and every picture had orbs in it. They were no reflective surfaced in the room so it wasn't the flash (creating the orb). The orbs were at head level over their shoulders," Jorgensen recalled.

They were quite excited about their findings, he added.

The Inn keeps a letter in the archives, written by a man in his 70s, about his paranormal experiences which happened to him as a boy in the 1940s.

"As the letter goes, the boy looked up at the staircase and saw a woman in a white dress beckoning him. He followed her down a hallway and all of a sudden a wall opened up and there was a hole with a light shining. She went into the hole beckoning him to come. As he started to come something banged him on the head and he fell down and frightened him so badly that he hid under the stairs until his mother found him a few hours later," finished Jorgensen.

Things that go bump in a Canadian night are rich with history and intrigue. Perhaps one day you will have experiences to share with your fellow readers.

CORNWALL & SEAWAY VALLEY TOURISM

Cornwall, On.

Prisons themselves are an extremely depressing place to be in. I'm not talking from experience, but prisons of yesteryear, where filled with agony, both the physical and mental types.

Not only were criminals placed in prisons but women and children along with handicapped, and emotionally challenged individuals were in these places of doom simply because their monetary providers were placed there.

Some prisons worked double duty as a poor house as well. At times the prisoners would hire people off the street to look after the inmates when the regular guards would go on break.

Some hired guards would have a field day of immoral activates when it came to the inmates. At times it really was up to the guard to inflict the punishment. Remember, this was more than 140 years ago. There were no cries of the prisoners who could reach the sympatric ears of the government.

The prisoners were considered lucky to survive another day only to live in almost inhuman conditions. For most inmates, they would die in prisons only to be buried nearby in unmarked graves. Their mental state might not have been the greatest upon entering prisons but one thing is for sure, if they did in fact leave with their lives, their mental state diminished only to have their anger fueled like a raging bonfire.

The District Courthouse and Gaol (TDCG) in Cornwall, On., is one of the oldest public structures in Ontario. The gaol is a landmark and has been in use as a courthouse since 1833.

The first building was built in 1802. The small building was measured at 30 feet by 24 feet.

When the War of 1812 broke out the court house was used as barracks. This war time measure forced the courts to open in the local

St. John's Church and neighborhood taverns.

In the winter of 1826 the building burned down making way to the second building which was built in 1833. It is the second building which has visitors of the past.

In 1833, a new court house and gaol was completed in the summer of 1833 at a total cost of 5,500 pounds (close to $15 million in today's standards).

Over the next 169 years many renovations were added to the historic structure.

In 2002, the jail was closed and it is currently in the possession of Cornwall & Seaway Valley Tourism. As of May 2005 tours are being offered to the history-interested public.

Barbara Matthews is the visitors services manager and general curator, for the past six years, who had experienced paranormal activity in the building.

"The first thing that happened to me was when I was walking down the hall to put the lights on and heard something like metal wheels on a trolley behind me. It kept getting louder and louder and closer and closer and when I turned around to look there was nothing there."

Unseen bodies could be heard whistling when no one was there; radios that would play music for 30 seconds and mysteriously turn off are just some of the experiences she had succumbed to over the years.

"There are more and more things happening all the time."

Although she does admit that she hasn't actually seen a spirit, she did hear cell doors slamming. Her desk is situated near the entrance and not in the jail itself. When the jail was visited by paranormal groups in the past and they did investigate the cell doors finding no evidence as to why the cell doors would slam.

Although the grounds are close to 200 years old, there were only five hangings there. The last hanging was in 1954. One year a fire broke out. Since the building was built on top of an army barrack, soldiers and animals perished in the flames. One part of the building was in fact built on top of a hanging yard where at least 200 bodies are laying.

Renay Dixon, visitor services assistant and tour guide of four years also works in the building that bumps in the night.

"When I was giving a tour, two other gentlemen we came across some really strong cigar smoke."

When she asked the men if they smelled the smoke "they looked at me as if I lost a couple of marbles."

There is a replica of the gallows in the jail and people would be taking pictures of the structure. "When they stepped in to the yard their digital cameras would stop working. Either their screens would freeze or their batteries would die," she stated.

Although she does believe the jail is haunted it doesn't make a difference when she goes to work. At times she does get the feeling the spirits doesn't want anyone in their jail.

Historic prisons are a great place not only for their history, but also for the things that go bump in a Canadian night.

OGOPOGO MONSTER
FACT OR FICTION

I must admit that while I did hear of Ogopogo, I never knew just what affect on the world Ogopogo really had.

Canada's most famous water monster is Ogopogo of Lake Okanagan in the south central interior of British Columbia. Although native legends support a monster living in Okanagan Lake long before white men arrived in this country, Ogopogo is very much a present day phenomenon.

Each year, sightings are reported of a creature some 20 to 50 feet long, with a horse shaped head and a body resembling a serpent. Okanagan Lake is about 80 miles long extending from Vernon at the north end to Penticton in the south with the fast growing city of Kelowna in the center. Sightings have been reported throughout the length of the lake but the monster appears to favour an area just south of Kelowna in waters near Peachland.

One of the first recorded sightings by a caucasion was by Mrs. John Allison in 1872 and such instances have continued to this day with many credible, rational and sober people becoming absolute believers. Native folklore specifically places the lair of the lake monster which they called N'ha-a-itk, or Lake Demon, at a cave under Squally Point near Rattlesnake Island which is offshore from Peachland.

It's been said that natives would never paddle a canoe near this area without an offering because too often a storm would spring up and N'ha-a-itk would rise out of the waters to claim another life. When white settlers first came to this area in the mid 1800s, they were not superstitious but gradually changed their views with ongoing sightings of the monster.

An early instance tells of two horses swimming behind a boat that were mysteriously pulled beneath the waves and the owner barely saving himself by cutting the rope attached to the horses. Today's sightings, often from modern power boats, indicate a much friendlier monster but still very large in size.

It has been filmed a number of times but other than people agreeing there was something in the water, no absolute conclusions have been made. It is usually reported as dark blue, black or brown with a lighter underside. It can move with astounding speed but many sightings in calm weather have been made of the creature apparently feeding on either fish or aquatic weeds. People very close, between 50 and 100 feet, report seeing fins or feet on the animal.

The first alleged film of the creature is The Folden Film, filmed in 1968 by Art Folden, which shows a dark object propelling itself through shallow water near the shore. The film was shot from on a hill above the shore.

Ogopogo was allegedly filmed again in 1989 by a used car salesman, Ken Chaplin, who with his father, Clem Chaplin, claimed to have seen a snake-like animal swimming in the lake, which flicked its tail to create a splash. Some believe that the animal the Chaplins saw was simply a beaver, because the tail splashing is a well-known characteristic of beavers. However, Chaplin alleges the animal he saw was 15 feet long, far larger than a typical beaver (beavers are approximately 4 feet (1.2 m) long). A few weeks later, Chaplin came back with his father and his daughter and filmed it again.

British cryptozoologistKarl Shuker has categorized the Ogopogo as a many hump variety of lake monster, and suggested it may be a kind of primitive serpentine whale such as Basilosaurus.

However, because the physical evidence for the beast is limited to unclear photographs and film, it has also been suggested that the sightings are misidentifications of common animals, such as otters, and inanimate objects, such as floating logs.

Another suggestion is that the Ogopogo is a lake sturgeon. It is also possible in some cases that Ogopogo could be the misidentification of a seiche, a standing wave in a lake that travels below the surface in a long serpentine motion.

Whatever Ogopogo really is it is forklore in a place we call Canada.

Ogopogo may not bump into buildings but if you go swimming in Lake Okanagan, this creature might, just might bump into you.

THE STRATFORD SHAKESPEARE FESTIVAL
Stratford On.

I was asked by my readers to expand on the Stratford Festival from my last episode into the paranormal. When I was asked to do this I was only too happy to comply. I enjoy taking requests and if you have or had a paranormal experience that happened in Canada, please email me at rwolf65@hotmail.com.

Now, turn the lights down low, snuggle deep into your favourite blanket and read if you dare the paranormal of Stratford Shakespeare Festival.

The Stratford Shakespeare Festival (SSF) is not only known for Shakespearian plays where Canadian actors received their huge breaks in the entertainment field.

Actors such as William Shatner and Christopher Plummer both received one of their first acting breaks here. Plummer still graces the stage with his larger-than-life presents here.

The festival is also known for spirits as well.

George the ghost is a familiar name to a lot of the staff noted Jay Klassen who was a head stage carpenter at the festival from 1988-2002.

"In the early days I was frequently there alone in the theater late at night. I heard noises, inexplicable noises and I could never find anybody and that raised the hair at the back off my neck a little bit," said Klassen during a telephone interview.

When he mentioned his experiences to another older employee he was told the strange tale of George who many believe was Ambrose Small who suddenly disappeared many years ago. Small owned a large chain of Vaudeville theaters in the early 1900s. For some reason Small was known as George.

The story goes that when the Avon was a cinema George was a janitor who was down on his luck and managed to make a small apartment in the theatre. The manager of the theatre was using the theater as a place for a rendezvous with someone's wife.

"George either stumbled across them or were aware of this going on and that the manager murdered him at the theater and that's why his spirit is on the prowl," recalled Klassen.

A lot of people working by themselves have heard noises, he said.

After the construction of 2000-01 of the Avon Theatre he never heard the noises again.

"After the reconstruction was completed, I no longer heard the noises. If there were any truth to the story, I guess the resting place of the ghost was sufficiently disturbed by them."

This article can't be officially closed without the Ghost Light.

"The Ghost Light is just a bare light bulb with a cage on it that stands on something like a coat rack. It has a base and a single pole. When you finish at night you bring it out onto the stage and leave it light until the next day. It's there so the ghosts are not in the dark," stated Nora Polley, archives assistant at the SSF.

The staff takes the ghosts at the festival very seriously. In the question of to be or not to be, some souls continue to be or at least still want to be. That is their final answer.

There are plenty more Canadian paranormal questions and answers and they will be reported in Things That Go Bump in a Canadian Night.

MACBETH'S CURSE

This story is a bit different than my previous stories. It's about a curse hundreds of years old. Believe it or not, it does have ties in Canada.

William Shakespeare was a playwright, poet, actor who died in 1616. He was not the Canadian actor who played Captain Kirk on Star Trek. That writer/actor was William Shatner.

Although their first names are the same and their initials are the same, the two actors and writers are not one of the same. So now we got that out of the way, we can start this true tale of what the men have in common and it's more that their initials.

Shakespeare wrote a play called Macbeth. The Tragedy of Macbeth (commonly called Macbeth) is a play about a regicide (the deliberate killing of a monarch, or the person responsible for the killing of a monarch) and its aftermath. It is Shakespeare's shortest tragedy and is believed to have been written sometime between 1603 and 1607.

In the back-stage world of theatre, some believe that the play is cursed, and will not mention its name aloud, referring to it instead as "The Scottish Play." Over the centuries, the play has attracted some of the greatest actors in the roles of Macbeth and Lady Macbeth.

    The play has been adapted to film, television, opera, novels, comic books, and other media. In 1604 Shakespeare in his zeal to please King James I, an authority on demonology, cast caution and imagination aside and for the opening scene of Macbeth's Act IV he reproduced a 17th century black-magic ritual, to budding witches. Remember, during this time people were still being burned as witches. Without changing an ingredient, Shakespeare provided his audience with step-by-step instructions in the furtive art of spell casting:

    "Round around the cauldron go; In the poison'd entrails throw. Toad, that under cold stone, Days and nights has thirty-one Swelter'd venum sleeping got. Boil thou first i' the charmed pot."

...And so on.

The ritual's practitioners were not amused by this detailed public exposure of their witchcraft, and it is said that as punishment they cast an everlasting spell on the play, turning it into the most ill-starred of all theatrical productions.

Over the years many actors suffered from the curse. During its 1849 performance at New York's Astor Place, a riot broke out in which 31 people were trampled to death. In 1934, British actor Malcolm Keen turned mute onstage, and his replacement, Alister Sim, (Scrooge) like Hal Berridge before him, developed a high fever and had to be hospitalized. In the 1942 Macbeth production headed by John Gielgud, three actors - Duncan and two witches - died, and the costume and set designer committed suicide amidst his devilish Macbeth creations.

So how does this have Canadian ties and how does Shatner fit in? In the town of Stratford, On. Stratford Shakespeare Festival has been attracting visitors since 1953.The festival is based on Shakespeare's plays and writings. Shatner got one of his first big breaks in the festival in the early 50s.

Even today, the Shakespeare festival walks on egg shells when it comes to the play Macbeth. They strongly honour the curse and refers to Macbeth as "the play" or "The Scottish Play." Stories about things that go bump in a Canadian night may not always have their start in Canada but they might have ties here.

THE LEGEND OF THE RINGING BELL
Charlottetown, P.E.I.

It was an event that had all the makings of a major Hollywood movie. Before global warming or the fear of the magic doomsday year of 2012 and way back in the dark cold days of October 1859 a bell rang out into the early morning hours. Those who heard the sound will never forget. St. James Church bell tower is the focal point and the building of this tale and the people of Charlottetown, P.E.I., are the players.

Why the ringing? It wasn't Sunday or a religious holiday, no one in their right mind would be married or buried in the early morning hours. Still the sound of the first ring of the bell rang out. When a second ring cried out into the stillness of the night two neighbours who heard the sound ran outside and met on the road. They joined forces and went to the source to investigate.

As they ventured forth, the bell continued to cry out its ringing. Was it ringing of doom or of joy? Only time will tell of the fate of the sleepy town. As the investigative team ventured into the courtyard, the bell rang out six times.

Like a scene in a Hollywood movie, the front doors of the church crashed open with a windy blast forcing the team to hit the ground by its shear blast. Before them were three glowing women all dressed in white. Angels of life or death? Angels to tell them of a future happenings or the sum of an event whose outcome will soon take place.

When the bell rang out for its seventh time, the heavy wooden doors slammed shut with the entities inside the church. The team rushed to the shut door and tried to open it but all was in vain. The door simply couldn't be open. Nothing on heaven or earth would open what was once opened by the three entities.

The team rushed to the windows to gain further information on what they seen. The three glowing women were seen walking upstairs to the belfry. Were they specters walking towards a bewitching event? The minister and the sexton (caretaker) arrived at the place of excitement and wanted to know what was going on at his church.

When the team told the newly arrived minister what they had seen the minister unlocked the doors and they ventured inside. Once inside the place of worship, none could see the three women anywhere. The bell was about to cry out one more time. As the team crept upwards towards the bell, the bell rang out its eighth and last time.

The brave team ran upstairs at this point to confront the intruders only to find nothing. Only the bell which they soon discovered was vibrating slightly. They were relieved that they were not the victims of mass hysteria but still bewildered on who, what or even why the bell tolled. Did it toll for them or perhaps the town itself? The church was investigated by the team. Every square inch of the building was searched.

They left no stone unturned. They simply couldn't find the answer behind what they seen or heard. That night, the Fairie Queen, a local steamer ship from Nova Scotia and Prince Edward Island, which was supposed to arrive in the nearby docks never showed. Her billowing clouds of black smoke, never seen. The answer to this mystery arrived a couple of days later.

If they had telephones or internet the answer would have come sooner. The bell which rang out eight times was for the eight victims, five men and three women, who perished from the sinking of the Fairie Queen.

If you suddenly got a chill from this tale then perhaps you will never hear a bell ring the same way again. Haunts, ghosts or even tales are told and retold in Things that Go Bump in a Canadian Night.

FORT SASKATCHEWAN MUSEUM AND HISTORIC SITE

We know that people were hanged in the past for their crimes. At times those who were executed didn't go all too willingly and their spirits may still be roaming the very grounds they had their last few moments on earth. Some spirits may like to play tricks on people while others like to take an evening stroll. Fort Saskatchewan Museum and Historic Site (FSMHS) is one of the jails that have seen some paranormal activities in its time. It was even on Creepy Canada, a Canadian TV show about the paranormal.

  The North-West Mounted Police (NWMP) established a fort on the south side of the North Saskatchewan River in 1875. When it was transferred to Edmonton in 1913, however, the old fort was destroyed, and a jail and courthouse went up in its stead. Established in 1958, the three-acre FSMHS is ideally located at heart of Fort Saskatchewan, near Legacy and Jarvis Parks and the historic CN Station.

At the site there are eight heritage buildings furnished with period pieces that form a picturesque historic village serenely overlooking the North Saskatchewan River and a collection focusing on the Northwest Mounted Police and the settlement era dating back to 1875.

Here are some quick facts on Fort Saskatchewan as researched by Fred Laudenklos, Historian. Between 1916 and 1960, 29 people were hanged at this jail. On execution days, only a few citizens recruited as witnesses, attended the hangings. These witnesses were recruited by the hangman and once chosen, were obligated to attend the hanging. In 1915 the $200,000 Provincial Jail building was completed. In 1919, a woman's jail was added, and an extension was built in 1921.

This case was featured in Creepy Canada a few years back. Emilio Picariello, 47, and Mary Florence Lassandro (aka/nee Filomena Costanzo and The Mobster

Princes), 23, were convicted of murdering Alberta Provincial Police Const. Steve Lawson, 42, in Coleman, Alta., on September 21, 1922. Lawson had recently fired a shot at Picariello's son, Steve, who was a rum-runner.

Steve suffered a minor injury. Picariello and Lassandro heard that Steve had been seriously, perhaps fatally, wounded and went to see Lawson. An argument followed and Lawson was shot in the back as he was returning to his house.

Picariello and Lassandro were hanged on May 2, 1923, at the Fort Saskatchewan Jail. Lassandro was the only woman hanged in Alberta and the fifth woman hanged in Canada. Lassandro claimed she was innocent right up to her execution. Before her execution an appeal went to Prime Minister William Lyon Mackenzie King but her appeals fell on deaf ears.

Years later a mock execution of Lassandro "looked so real that I almost threw up," noted Sandy McArdle, vice-president of the FSMHS.

Years ago, a woman worked in the courthouse. Just across the hall from her was a bathroom and she was the only one in the building. She was typing away and the light switch in the bathroom came on. She went into the bathroom and found the switch turned on so she turned the switch off. It kept reoccurring so an electrician was called and everything checked out fine.

There was no reason for the mysterious incident. "She quit because of the ghost in there."

According to the Creepy Canada episode, Irene Martina, a clairvoyant and medium entered the courtroom with a pendulum to seek out the spirits there. She discovered a strong thick atmosphere and cold spots near the judge's bench. Later when Martina investigated the Dr. Henry House she picked up the spirits of two children and his wife. Martina stated that it was this house that had the most spiritual energy in the fort.

Darlene Briere is a volunteer of special events and programs and also of research stated that she experienced strange happenings, voices and noises along with shapes and images of people. One year, there was a Halloween event called Fright Night at the museum's grounds. Briere was taking a stroll on the jail's grounds and a fog rolled in.

There were no clouds in the sky. When she took a picture of the fog, an image of a woman appeared in the fog in the picture. "I strongly believe it was the image of Florence," the woman who was executed. Later that evening Briere went to do a second check on the buildings and noted a curtain was moving in one of the rooms. The curtain "crumpled" to the floor. When she lifted the curtain up she witnessed a face that of a young lady. "We got more than we bargained for when we participated that night," she said.

WASHINGTON AVENUE GRILL

I've said it many times that ghosts and spirits can haunt anything they want to. As far as science is concerned we do not have anything to prevent them to haunt the buildings and places they of their out worldly choosing.

Today, we go back to Vancouver, B.C., and look in on Washington Avenue Grill, which is a fine dining establishment, with a history to tell.

"There's always a lot of things happening that no one can explain like things falling over and noises and there never seems to be a reason for it happening. I haven't seen anything. I have people that have seen really odd things happening around the restaurant," said Brent Grey, owner.

"We've been here for 13 years and it's been going on since we've been here."

There is a graveyard that can be seen from the restaurant windows. One of the workers have seen "something come out of the ground, up our stairs and in to the restaurant."

The bathroom seems to be a point of haunting events. A customer saw "someone in the mirror (a spirit) and said, 'I won't be coming back to your restaurant.'"

He thinks that some people are meant to see the spirits while others are not or perhaps they are just slow to see them.

Alarms that go off in the middle of the night when no one is around are just another example of the paranormal activities which the restaurant is host to.

A coffee pot handle would fly off the pot while the pot was sitting. Others felt someone (not seen) behind them or rush past them. One time a few people were downstairs and the lights would dim down and would come back on again, one of the workers stated.

A few weeks ago half of the wine bottles fell down but no one has touched them for the past four hours. They smashed on the ground and almost hit a few people.

"I had to change the garbage in the women's washroom and when I went to open one of the doors someone was pushing against it. So I waited a couple of minutes for someone to come out and nothing happened. I waited a few minutes and when the door opened no one was inside noted Chloe Trudel, an employee for about three months. Trudel said things seem to break a lot for no appear reason. One of her friends would barley touch something and it would explode.

A legend is written on the back of the desert menu read by Trudel. It reads as follows:

Arthur Sharp 1934. Built in 1913 The Campbell River Lumber Company the building was originally a lumber mill which employed over 400 workers to cut lumber to produce building trenches in Russia during the First World War. It had many uses over the years among them a Presbyterian Church, a school, and housed to migrant railway workers.

In 1934 after the mill shut down it became the home of Sharp who acted as a caretaker for the building and the surrounding land. Sharp was a quiet man who kept to himself never venturing into town. During a stormy night in November 1943, locals remember hearing strange screams of pain echoing through the hills. Sharpe was never to be seen again. Some people claim he was struck by a train.

Some say he drowned during a late evening swim; others say he went crazy and locked himself in the buildings rafters. It is now believed that the old caretaker roams the grounds today in spirit. There have been many reports of odd occurrences. Items have been moved and noises have been heard in the ceilings and walls. Some people claim to have seen the caretakers' shadow lurking around the building.

Spirits may have a hunger to haunt restaurants and their employees. Perhaps this story should be on the first page of a paranormal menu and the restaurant simply called Things That Go Bump In a Canadian Night.

A TALE OF TWO RESTAURANTS
Burlington, On.

Haunted stories, tales, or events; call them what you will but this particular story really started way back in the late 1800s. British Loyalists Emma and George Byren came to this new land called Canada.

They opened a restaurant in 1902 called Estaminet. Although the history of the restaurant is extremely rare and newspaper articles are few and far between we do know that according to Patrick Cross and Michelle Desrochers', website burlingtonghostwalks.ca In 1943 Emma celebrated her 70th birthday at the Estaminet. Emma ran the well known establishment until it was sold. It has since changed hands several times up until 1994 when it became known as Emma's Back Porch (EBP) Restaurant. This is the longest running restaurant in Ontario.

But not all tales or stories have good times and this one of forgotten lore is no exemption. It seems the Byren's had five children two of which passed into the great beyond at an earlier age. Robert died when he was six years old playing near the water as he slipped on rocks while Sahara died at the age of four of pneumonia. Perhaps it is these children which can be seen and heard to this very day at the restaurant.

Mike Crooks, manager of the EBP for the last eight years, retold a particular story which seems to back up the information that children do in fact haunt the restaurant. Could it be Robert?

Before Crooks' arrival as manager, Fred (not real name) was hired as a dishwasher in 1994. Fred went downstairs to get ice cream from the old walk-in freezer. He came up stairs and went home. He only worked for one hour. The reason for his early departure was a child was sitting downstairs. When Fred went to see if the child was OK, Fred's hand went right through the child, stated Crooks.

Crooks research into this particular story backed-up the story of a young employee that went home after one hour of employment.

If anyone knows anything about the restaurant it would be Pat Cross. He investigated the legend for well over a year and there's more information being found as time goes by. Although Cross could not be reached in time for this article, his partner in paranormal spoke on his behalf.

"Emma spent a lot of time greeting people on the stairs," stated Michelle Desrochers, one of the directors at Burlington Ghost Walks which is a division of Canada's Most Haunted Research.

It was on the fourth step that Emma died. Some people would feel sick on the unlucky step and others feel a little push. One true and unfortunate episode happened on the very step. An elderly woman felt that she was pushed on the fourth step causing her to fall, causing internal bleeding from which she perished a week later, she noted.

Desrochers had her own episode of the paranormal while giving a tour there. She said she stopped in the washroom while the tour ventured on.

"I could hear footsteps coming but I couldn't hear anything after that. I could hear this door close. I raced out of the bathroom. I opened the door because they would have been in the main part of the foyer. They would be no way they would be gone that fast. There was nobody there at all."

When it comes to those that bump in the paranormal there are untold theories on spirits but one theory most people seem to agree on.

"Time is completely irrelevant. The cycle of the moon, the earth, all that, they're energy based not so much time based," she explained.

Some of the famous which visited the restaurant include: Ella Fitzgerald, Liberace, Former Prime Ministers John Diefenbaker, and Pierre Elliott Trudeau. There were rumours that Queen Elizabeth visited the restaurant in the 1940s before she become the queen.

Another incident includes that of an old industrial salad spinner. It takes two adult hands to spin the spinner. At times it can be seen spinning by itself.

Lastly, just few weeks ago, another incident happened in the basement of the restaurant a.k.a the dungeon, while cleaning junk from the basement. At the end of the night one of the managers and bartenders heard some "freaky noises" glasses shaking, static sounds, pounding sounds on the walls and floors while the girls were finishing off their shifts. They would be the first to make light of what others might have seen or heard. They both were adamant about what they both heard enough to freak them out. They are still nervous about being downstairs, stated Crooks.

Burlington Ghost Walks start their tours at EBP. "It's a two-hour-tour just like Gillian's Island." At times the tours even go longer depends on what we find there, ended Desrochers.

CASA LOMA

There is a landmark which most Torontonians know about; it's called

Casa (a.k.a Castle) Loma (CL). It was built by Major-General Sir Henry Mill Pellatt, (January 6, 1859 - March 8, 1939) was a well-known Canadian financier and soldier and for his role in bringing hydro-electricity to Toronto for the first time.

In 1903 Pellatt purchased 25 lots from developers Kertland and Rolf. Pellatt commissioned Canadian architect E.J. Lennox to design (CL) with construction beginning in 1911, starting with the massive stables, potting shed and Hunting Lodge (a.k.a coach-house) a few hundred feet north of the main building.

The Hunting Lodge is a two storey 4,380 square foot house with servant's quarters. As soon as the stable complex was completed, Pellatt sold his summer house in Scarborough to his son and moved to the Hunting Lodge.

The stables were used as a construction site for the castle (also served as the quarters for the men servants), with some of the machinery still remaining in the rooms under the stables.

The house cost approximately $3.5 million ($75.79 million today) and took a team of 300 workers three years to build from start to finish. During the Second World War, CL was used to conceal research on sonar and for construction of sonar devices (known as ASDIC) for U-boat detection. Some of the unique features CL has are: an oven large enough to cook an ox, two secret passages, three never completed bowling alleys and ghosts.

Michelle Desrochers, one of the directors at Burlington Ghost Walks which is a division of Canada's Most Haunted Research.

It is a legitimate research organization and registered company going into their ninth year, she said.

"The staff members have always known it (CL being haunted). They kept it quite for a very long time."

Since the world-wide interest in haunting, they have decided to come forward and tell the world the place is truly haunted.

In most cases paranormal groups approach the haunted sites.

"They basically approached us. We never made any inquiries about it. We were very surprised to get a phone call."

We just completed an article for Toronto Life which is a very prestigious magazine in Toronto."

"We were honoured and thrilled all at once" when CL approached us. "It's a very, very historical phenomenal place."

Lady in White is an example of the paranormal which occurs at CL. We don't know too much about her only that she looks "very serious, looking very stern" a few people have her on film but never sent any pictures into CMH. There's a man in the tunnel. We have voice recordings of him, she said.

Once in the tunnel last October, with three other members, she heard and felt something from beyond this world.

I could feel something cold from the side of my face and heard a huge " why," she stated.

The next day she went down alone. She asked the darkness, hoping to get a response from the spirit, "so you don't like the idea of cameras," she asked. "Why, why" were the sounds she heard again. She said that she has the voice on recording.

"We got a lot of evidence out of there. Last week a woman got a photo of a spirit woman sitting on the bed in Lady Mary's (Pellatt) Room.

"It was fantastic because you could see a major distortion and you could see the bun on her head and she was a heavy set woman" just like Lady Mary. "It was just amazing."

Ghost and spirits haunt everything from the poorest of places to the richest of properties. They never discriminate and neither does

Things That Go Bump In a Canadian Night.

MCKAY AVENUE SCHOOL
Edmonton, Alta.

Once in a while there is truly a strange haunting that it must be reported on. You'll know what I mean as you read this strange case. It was on this month 104 years ago that the McKay Avenue School in Edmonton opened its doors to students and spirits.

The school had reports of being haunted soon after it was built in 1905. At the time mysterious voices could be heard near the two-stone fireplaces. Usually, it takes years if not decades after a building is made when it becomes haunted if at all.

Other occurrences include the traditional haunting events: locked doors become unlocked, furniture being mysteriously moved, wooden floors being scraped, lights being turned on. All these events are done by unseen hands of those from the netherworld.

The following events are taken from Beware of Ghosts at McKay Avenue School (published in April 2002) by Mike Kostek, Archivist, EPS Archives & Museum.

Ron Hlady, former custodian and building preservation technician, has had his own encounters. Frank Newson, a former student and public school trustee in the early years of the 20th century, recalled the strangest event this reporter ever heard.

It seems a student got stuck in a crawl space in the bowels of the school. Although he was rescued alive his screams could still be heard. It was not an echo of his screams; his screams could be heard for years after. Enter the 1960s and a former school principal George Schurman recalls moaning sounds from the school's attic. About 86 years after the school was built, Ena Schneider, a secretary at the school, said that something strange would brush past her on several incidents.

Another employee John McCormick, painter, said something tried to push him off his ladder not once but on several occasions. Finally, a team of respected psychics spent the night in the school trying to contact some, if not all, of the spirits which make the old school their home.

Each member of the team had encounters with the tenants from another dimension. They are in fact owners of photos of weird shapes as the shapes hovered over the old wooden staircase.

Katherine Luck, Supervisor of Edmonton Public School Archives and Museums, stated that at around the Halloween season many paranormal groups who explore the unknown "are convinced" that the building has spirits which roam the halls and rooms.

One personal incident Luck recalls involved a radio station. After one paranormal group packed up their equipment and left the building she turned on her car radio on her way home. The station CBC was on 730AM instead of 740AM.

"I couldn't get it on 740AM."

Luck said she turned off her radio and about a half mile away from the school "I turned it on again and it went to 740AM."

"I'm not convinced but I'm not 'unconvinced'," she stated about her experience, the spirits and strange incidents about the school.

The 78-year-old building closed in 1983 and reopened the same year as an archive and museum where it is in operation today.

There is really no time limit whether a building is haunted. The land itself can be haunted, making whatever structure built on the land haunted as well. Young ghosts or old spirits, they all have a place to haunt in Things That Go Bump in a Canadian Night.

CANADIAN HORROR MOVIES

This article is dedicated for those about to travel into the dark zone of horror movies. These are some of my favourite horror movies which happen to be filmed in Canada.

The first movie on my list is Black Christmas (1974). The film made me almost jump out of my skin each time the phone rang. I must caution you the phone conversations have strong offensive language even by today's standards.

Working from a budget of $620,000 it grossed $4,053,000. It is one of the first movies where a killer stalks and kills college students. Canadian actors Keir Dullea, Margot Kidder, John Saxon, Andrea Martin, Doug McGrath, Art Hindle and Argentina-born Olivia Hussey star in the classic movie.

The next film The Changeling (1980) is another great Canadian film. George C. Scott and his real wife Trish Van Devere stars in this ghost film. Scott stars as Dr. John

Russell, a composer living in New York City, who moves cross-country to Washington state following the tragic deaths of his wife and daughter in a traffic accident while on a winter vacation in upstate New York. In suburban Seattle, Russell rents a Victorian-era mansion and begins piecing his life back together.

However, Dr. Russell soon discovers that he has unexpected company in his new home when a poltergeist, the ghost of a murdered child, haunts the house. Russell investigates and finds that the mystery is linked to a powerful local family, the heir of whom is a wealthy US senator.

In one scene Russell uses a tape recorder to tape a séance and picks up the voice of a dead child loud and clear (wish it was that easy). This is a perfect family horror movie because it contains no nude scenes, no gore or strong offensive language. The movie was filmed at the University of Toronto and Vancouver, This film was #54 on Bravo's 100 Scariest Movie Moments.

The movie Videodrome (1983) is another piece of Canadian horror. Although a bit dated, it stars Debbie Harry, James Woods and Canadian Sonja Smits. The film scored fourth as Bravo TV's 30 Even Scarier Movie Moments. The movie was filmed in Toronto and the budge was just under six million dollars and it grossed only $2,120,439.

The movie is about Max Renn (Woods) a TV station president, who finds a satellite TV show from Asia. He tries to pirate the show but finds weird events which surround the show. He meets Nicki Brand, a radio announcer (Harry), who leads him astray and gets him into a "hurt locker" of sorts. This movie is not a family movie. Strong language and other scenes including "tasteful gore" make it into this movie.

QUEEN'S PARK: ONTARIO LEGISLATIVE BUILDING

Toronto, On.

You can call them ghosts or spirits. To most of the living it makes very little difference but what about to them? The next time I interview a ghost or spirit I will ask them.

As for this article, let's call them ghosts. Even politicians are not immune from these ghosts from another time and or dimension. Queens Park is the area of this haunting while the 117-year- old Ontario Legislative Building (OLB) is the place.

According to the out-of-print publication Grandeur, Ghosts and Gargoyles which was printed in the late 1970s and distributed by the Legislative Assembly.

In the early days (at the building), the ghosts appeared. Frank Yeigh, author and journalist who wrote the only definitive history of the building (at the time), kept notes on them in his files, which are now in the Ontario Archives.

An old soldier, in full regimental dress, was said to parade in the office of the Queen's Printer. There were three women inmates of the old asylum – one in white with streaming hair, one wearing a checked dress thrown over her head and one who had hanged herself in the basement.

All were said to make distressing moans. One night watchman refused to enter the reporters' room after dark because of the noise. They have not been heard of since the turn of the century.

The previous information was send to me by David Bogart, Parliamentary Protocol and Public Relations.

Before the OLB was built in 1893, the land was used as the University Lunatic Asylum (official title).

The reasoning of the name might have been that the asylum was on the university grounds. The origins of the site go back to Kings College which became University of Toronto.

The province took the land over in the 1850s thinking that it would be used to construct a new parliament in which it did.

The area was to be used as the new national capital, but it turned out to be in Ottawa. When the building wasn't used as the new national building, it was used as a hospital which is now the OLB. The old lease of 999 (666 upside down and the building is haunted. Could there be some kind of coincidence?) years no longer exists.

Bogart said, "that lease was over in 1880 when the province acquired the land and became an official accusation in 1894. The lease had to do with the city and the university and not the province."

To quote Toronto Sun columnist Christina Blizzard in her article *The hallowed, haunted halls The ghosts of Queen's Park* harken back to a time when it really was an asylum.

The White Lady wanders the halls, appearing sorrowful, with a long white flowing robe and long hair. The Maiden wears a checkered dress with an apron which she holds over her face to conceal her features.

Most gruesome is The Hanging Woman, who dangles from a hook in the long tunnel in the basement. Also here is a curious (and probably recent) apparition of a soldier in full regimental dress who appears angry as he descends the Grand Staircase of the main hall.

The chills start when you descend through the clutter and junk into the damp vault.

I personally believe that since that Canadian ghosts don't vote, they don't care where they haunt.

OXFORD COUNTY COURTHOUSE
Oxford, On.

Research can be an extremely fickle task at best. Sometimes, research can fall into your hands while at times great research can be confusing leaving you with nothing in the long run.

But if you are lucky heroes can happen at the most crucial times when you are pulling your hair out.

Mary Gladwin and Ernie Hunt are the heroes of this article and without their great assistance this article would have surely found a home in the garage can.

The first court house in the 'county', actually District of Brock, was built circa 1842. The building was located on what we call County Square, but a bit in front of the location of the current Court House", stated Gladwin, Archivist for the County of Oxford Archives.

This building contained both administrative offices and gaol (jail) but was eventually deemed inadequate and a new gaol was constructed in the mid-1850s, with a new Court House being erected in the early 1890s, she continued.

A local ghost at the court house might be that of Thomas Cook. Cook was convicted of the murder of his wife Bridget Morin and was executed in 1862. We understand that his head was severed (when the rope tightened) and rolled down into the audience, noted Gladwin.

"I understand that it was after this that people reported seeing Thomas searching for his head."

From what I have heard, the building that is haunted is the current court house, but the building was not there when these two men who are thought to haunt it, were hanged, she added. As with many old buildings, there are little nooks and crannies; there are creaky walls, especially when there is a strong wind (or perhaps there are bats in the attic); and lights often flicker.

A small elevator was built to provide accessibility and it has many quirks. Sometimes, it heads up to the top floor even if no one has programmed it for that; sometimes, it heads down to the ground floor all for no known reason.

Ernie Hunt was in charge of the court house renovations in 1981.

"We laid our supplies out for a Saturday morning early start for plumbing in one of the washrooms. Most of the parts were missing the next morning. We had no break-ins, we had cleaning staff until 1 a.m.", recalled Hunt.

Pictures were taken during the renovations and an important picture went missing. As well, an image of a face appeared in one of the pictures.

It made so many rounds that it never came back."

Even in the study of the paranormal, there are heroes in things that go bump in a Canadian night.

THE OLD GUELPH JAIL
Guelph, On.

When you think of old jails you would probably think of inmates wearing striped prison outfits hooked up to a ball and chain as they pulverize boulders into gravel. You would not be too far off from the truth.

The Guelph Correctional Centre (GCC) a.k.a the Guelph Reformatory, started construction in the first decade of the 20th century and didn't really finish until about 60 years later in the 1970s.

A paranormal investigation took place on November 25, 2007 at the GCC.

"We were working with YTV's show 'Ghost Trackers' at the time and they had asked us to come in and conduct a preliminary investigation to better find out what was going on there in regards to paranormal activity. We had asked Wanda Hewer, a psychic from Guelph to join us for the investigation too," Stephanie Cumerlato, co-founder of Haunted Hamilton said.

A two-hour tour filled the first part of the investigation, she said.

"Then darkness started to creep in. The long hallways started to feel like they were closing in on us. The air became heavy and mysterious. The fact that 'Ghost Trackers' was filming there was pretty neat too, because they had their purple spot lights set up all around the building, casting an eerie purple glow.

It was an overwhelming feeling that became even more intense as it got darker and darker. It almost felt like the prisoners were still there, trapped inside the jail forever."

Cumerlato said she saw something which made her stop in her tracks.

There were several incidents which have occurred that night.

"One incident that stands out in my mind was when we were walking through the infirmary area. I was the first one up the steps and was met by a long hallway with a bunch of doors on either side," she noted.

"I quickly saw a black shadow dart from one room to the other, across the hall. That scared me enough to not want to venture any further so the rest of the team had proceeded a bit further until we all got the sense that we shouldn't be in there. We looked around a few rooms and then left the area immediately.

"But before we did, there was one patient room that both Wanda and I stepped into. She started pacing in a circle and said that she was picking up on a spirit in there that was very nervous and anxious. Maybe he was waiting for a procedure to be done?"

"We're not sure. But Wanda did sense that he was torn up about something. He (the spirit) couldn't sit still because of the pain."

"All in all, the location is definitely haunted, not by one, but many spirits that are still trapped there," Cumerlato finished.

The GCC is just one haunted experience in Ontario that is being taken extremely serious in the paranormal realm.

VICTORIA GOLF CLUB
Victoria, B.C.

Things or those who go bump in a Canadian night are not limited to buildings. They can in fact haunt just about anything or anywhere they chose. This world is their playground or in this case, their golf course.

Victoria Golf Club, located at 1110 Beach Drive Victoria, B.C., was established in 1893. It is the oldest golf club in Canada and is still on its original site, overlooking the Strait of Juan de Fuca in the Municipality of Oak Bay.

The club is home to some 1,150 golfing and social members. The 35,000 sq. ft. clubhouse was completely renovated and updated in 1993. It is open year-round and offers a wide range of casual and fine dining facilities for receptions, large dinner dances and other special events. Some of these events might just be of the paranormal kind.

On September 22, 1936 Doris Gravlin a 30-year-old nurse went out for a stroll one night by her separated husband Victor, a hard-drinking journalist husband. It's not clear as to why they were out for a late night walk on the 7th fairway but one thing is certain. Her body was found under some logs severely beaten and strangled by the hands of Victor. Victor committed suicide by taking a stroll into the ocean.

A caddy at the club found her body five days later, while Victor's body exactly four weeks later, was found floating in a bed of kelp just off the shore of the golf course with her shoes in his pockets.

With the discovery of Victor's body, the case was officially closed as a murder-suicide.

"Her ghost is considered the most frequently seen ghost in this area. People who go ghost hunting will probably look for her ghost, "stated *John Adams of Ghostly Walks Tours, Victoria, B.C.

"She appears as a figure in white moving very quickly towards you and then veering away and suddenly disappearing or running circles around groups of people and then basically pinning them inside her circle. She sometimes appears as a large globe of light which will move and fly up over you. She sometimes appears as a figure that runs and flies up in the air. She has been seen ever since her murder in 1936."

About a year ago, grandparents had their grandchildren Billy and Lisa (not real names) visit from out of town. John (not real name) took his grandson Billy fishing down by the rocky sea shore. John received a fish hook in the head and the two went to the emergency ward at the nearby hospital.

Billy informed his grandfather that they forgot the tackle box. Later the four of them grandpa, grandma and two grandchildren went out to retrieve the box. After the two men got the box, they saw a figure in white heading towards them rather quickly. Suddenly the figure jumped up and flew over them. They then saw the figure running towards the edge of the golf course then looping back towards the car.

By the time they got back to the car Lisa was in hysterics since she had seen the figure as well. The grandparents knew who the figure was and all four seen the ghost, explained Adams.

If you ever play the seventh fairway call "fore" twice. Once for the people you can see and once for those that go bump in a Canadian night.

*John Adams, one of Victoria's foremost historians and storytellers, who has been leading ghost tours through the alleys and haunted places of Victoria since 1970. He has appeared on the TV series Ghosts and Ghoulies and on OLN's Creepy Canada. The tours are conducted by John and his team of expert guides.

FORT GARY HOTEL
Winnipeg, Man.

This week we visit a hotel fit for a queen and king and those that bump in a night.

Famous people who were patrons of the hotel include Nelson Eddy, Harry Belafonte, Charles Laughton, Lawrence Olivier, Liberace, Arthur Fiedler, Louis Armstrong, Gordie Howe, Lester Pearson, as well as King George VI and Queen Elizabeth, who stayed during their 1939 visit to Canada.

The construction of the hotel, situated on 222 Broadway Ave. Winnipeg, Man., started in September 1911 and finished December 1913 by the Grand Trunk Pacific Railway. It is located one block from the railway's Union Station, and was the tallest structure in the city when it was completed. Presently it is run as an independent hotel.

Room 202 and the rest of the majestic Fort Gary Hotel are reported to be haunted. It may sound like a Hollywood movie but these reports are not new, the reports stem back sever decades.

There are many stories of the hotel and the dark room of 202. One story consists of a bride and her unfortunate honeymoon.

A bride haunts the room. Her husband died in room 202, said Sherraine Christopherson, director of sales and marketing for Fort Gary Hotel.

"I had one experience a few years ago that made me believe. I had a young eight year-old boy stay with me from the U.S. from Make A Wish Foundation. His wish was to see the polar bears."

He was in the bedroom and he took some pictures outside the door and took some pictures in the bedroom. About a month later or more I spoke to his parents. His mother was telling me some of the pictures on the film that they took didn't come out. The ones that didn't come out were the three taken in the bedroom and two outside the door, said Christopherson.

Out of the 36 pictures only those five didn't come out "so it made you think, you know what I mean."

What happened to the film is very common when apparitions appear on film. Spirits are not a big fan of their picture being taken.

As I said previously, there are many reports of the hotel being haunted and room 202 is just one of them. There is just so much I can fit in this column so I can only briefly describe the rest. In the main dining room a phantom guest can be seen. On the second floor of the hotel strange lights and noises can be seen and heard. Deep within the bowels of the hotel's basement a hole in the foundation emanates eerie sounds and figures, throughout the hotel, simply disappear into thin air.

The hotel's website is a treasure chest of information including these statistics. The hotel height is 192 feet, or 14 stories; in 1913 the cost of the hotel was $1.5 million CDN today $25 million CDN ; 2.8 million bricks; 3,000 tons of steel; 4,900 cubic yards of concrete; 70,000 square yards of plaster and six to seven miles of plumbing pipe.

Things that go bump in Canadian night simply doesn't haunt only majestic buildings, they haunt anything and everything.

GLOSSARY OF GHOST HUNTING TERMS

There are many TV shows, books, magazines, radio programs about the paranormal. In these various types of media, they may use lots of terminology that are difficult to understand.

When reading, watching or listening about the paranormal, keeping this handy list of terminology as a guide, will make your experiences a lot easier to understand when we travel in things that go bump in a Canadian night.

Apparition - Since the early 17th century, this refers to any ghost that seems to have material substance. If it appears in any physical form, including a vapor-like image, it may be called an apparition.

Banshee - From the Irish, bean sidhe, meaning female spirit. Her wail does not always mean death, and she does not cause anyone to die. She's generally not a ghost.

Ectoplasm - Often referred to as "ecto," this is the physical residue of psychic energy. It's the basis for "slime" used in the Ghostbusters movies. Ectoplasm can be seen by the naked eye, and is best viewed in dark settings since it is translucent and tends to glow. It is very unusual.

Entity - Any being, including people and ghosts.

EVP - Electronic Voice Phenomena, or the recording of unexplained voices, usually in haunted settings. You can pick up a voice recorder at any electronic store or eBay.

Ghost - A sentient entity or spirit that visits or lingers in our world, after he or she lived among us as a human being. We've also seen evidence of ghostly animals and pets.

Haunted - Describes a setting where ghosts, poltergeists, and/or residual energy seem to produce significant paranormal activity. The word "haunt" originally meant to frequent.

Medium - Someone who can communicate between our world and the other side.

Occult - From the Latin, meaning something that is concealed or covered. Since the 16th century, it has meant anything that is mysterious.

Orb - A round, whitish or pastel-colored translucent area in photos. Generally, these are perfectly circular, not oval. Many researchers believe that they represent spirits or ghosts.

Paranormal - The prefix, "para" indicates something that is irregular, faulty, or operating outside the usual boundaries. So, "paranormal" refers to anything outside the realm and experiences that we consider normal.

Psi - Popular term used to mean any psychic phenomena, psychic abilities, and sometimes inclusive of paranormal disturbances as well.

Residual energy - Many ghost hunters believe that emotionally charged events leave an imprint or energy residue on the physical objects nearby.

Spirit - This word comes from the Latin word, meaning that which breathes. It means that which animates life, or the soul of the being.

THE OLD DON JAIL
Toronto, On.

Many old buildings appear eerie or haunted but there's one in Ontario that has its share of sad times and of haunted stories.

It was this month, 146 years ago that Don Jail a.k.a "Palace for Prisoners" opened for business.

In 1864 prisoners worldwide had been confined in appalling and inhumane conditions, such as three or four inmates to a cell with a bucket for a toilet that was emptied once a day.

Even though the conditions at the jail were better than before, they still were horrendous by today's standards. The jail saw 34 executions and even women and children that were locked away with the man of the family, a suicide, and a least one famous haunting.

The famous haunting is that of a young woman with blonde hair. It was there, in one of the tiny cells reserved for women in the west wing, that a prisoner hanged herself in the 1890s.

She's about 5' 6", wears a white gown and appears very agitated as she floats up around the second level of the rotunda, said field investigator Scott Smith of Toronto. Ghosts and Hauntings Research Society with more than 25 years of experience.

It was reported that jail guards on the graveyard shift saw her spirit floating through the air in the main *rotunda.

The power of suggestion is huge when it comes to the paranormal. A few years back in Toronto a group of people invented the Phillip Experiment.

"They created their own ghost. They made up a history for this gentleman, a name Phillip, a location, a lot of information creating this person. They had a séance and this person came by and talked to them."

From all the people in the group they had created an entity. It was a hugely wonderful experience "One important thing to remember when investigating is if the ghost experience is real. If someone said they had seen a ghost they believe it. I take every bit of information they give me but it's not a case of whether I can prove a ghost exists or that they saw what they believe they saw. It's a case of what caused them to see it. That's what I'm interested in."

Other events include a punching bag being punched from ghostly hands. One person, according to the website www.torontoghosts.org, was taking a tour of the jail, had strange experiences.

"While standing in one particular area outside a row of cells in the east wing, the air began to feel heavy and I experienced a chill, a tingling sensation on my skin and an overwhelming sense of sadness."

Recently 15 men who went to the gallows between 1880 and 1932 were uncovered on a TV show "The Hangman's Graveyard."

The Don Jail closed its cell doors for good in 1977. No matter if the living has been good or bad or how long ago their voyage was on earth, some spirits never leave. Their lives become a huge part in things that go bump in a Canadian night.

* The rotunda was used in the movie Cocktail as the movie's main bar.

FIDDLER'S GREEN IRISH PUB

Fiddler's Green Irish Pub, located in Cambridge, On., comes complete with its resident ghosts. Emily is the star of this legend, which started almost 100 years ago.

Back in 1885, a post office was built (now Fiddler's Green Irish Pub) in Galt, On. (now part of Cambridge). Thomas Fuller designed the post office (Fuller also designed the Parliament Building in Ottawa).

William S. Turnbull, was a postmaster from 1898-1919. He was secretly in love with a fellow postal employee known only as Emily (last name unknown). No one knows if William insisted to keep their affair a secret or tried to end it but nevertheless, Emily threatened to publicize their love affair. This action would have ruined Turnbull as a postmaster.

A few days later Emily's lifeless body was found in the rafters of the clock tower. Was it suicide or murder? A few weeks later, Turnbull died in his sleep. Was it a broken heart, suicide, or murder that ended his life as well?

To this very day, strange sightings and ghostly apparitions appear at Fiddler's Green. It must be noted here that several customers have apparently spotted the ghost of a young man and a young woman.

The third floor is called Emily's Attic Dance Club, named after Emily herself.

One of the managers, Todd, (requested to keep his last name unknown) recalled one night at 9 p.m. when a bottle of gin levitated from behind the bar, began spinning in mid air, flew across the floor only to smash into countless pieces.

Other unworldly experiences include chairs bounced with the aid of unseen individuals, lights dimmed by themselves, and water taps turning off and on after they have been tightly turned off. The pool room door has been known to open when a staff member securely locked it.

The third floor, where Emily's hanged body was found; windows were screwed shut only to be found opened. People have claimed to have seen mysterious black shadows pass by the upper windows and even a face that actually appears to form in the clock itself.

It is known that in 1991, when the building was called Time Club, a séance was done by a psychic. In the séance they have seemed to contact Turnbull's spirit who also seemed to haunt the building. It is unknown if their spirits still linger on at Fiddler's green Irish Pub but one thing is for sure, there will always be things that go bump in a Canadian night.

ROGERS' CHOCOLATES
Victoria, B.C.

If a successful business is old enough and lasts the passing of time it very well may have seen great happiness and great sorrow. This happens to be true in the case of Rogers' Chocolates.

Charles "Candy" Rogers (1855-1927) was born in Petersham, Mass. and as a teenager made his way across the US working on the railroad. He came across into Canada through New Westminster, B.C. in 1881 and worked as a logger before making his way to Victoria, B.C.

When he opened his grocery store in 1885 he began to sell candy. The candy was so good that it was outselling his groceries. Rogers developed his own candy recipe and Rogers's chocolates were born.

Another birth arrived in the next decade when, in 1888 Rogers married Leah Morrison (1864-1952) and together shared great happiness when their son Frederick Morrison Rogers (1890-1905) was born. Great sorrow occurred in 1905 when Fredrick committed suicide at 15 years old.

Bodiless hand prints on the glass and a child, possibly Fredrick, can be heard laughing. When someone heard the laughter they stated it was a boy's laughter so it would make sense that it would be Fredrick, said Mark Harrison, manager.

"Only two of the staff actually heard him at different times, like months apart so it's a real happening," noted Harrison.

Over the years chocolates would be thrown at him about 8-12 times. One of the staff members seen chocolates rise three feet off the shelf and onto the floor.

"I've seen the Red Rogers boxes fall off the shelves with no tremors, no nothing just like dominos. There were all genuine experiences in the last seven years," Harrison stated.

One time he came out of the washroom and heard sounds of someone running up and down the 106 year-old wooden floors with high heels.

"If you think I was coming out your wrong. I locked the door and I refused to come out for anybody. I stayed in there for a good five minutes," he said laughingly.

When he did come out, nobody was there.

About six months ago, a staff member approached him when he came to work asking if he was in earlier because she heard sounds of someone running upstairs with high heels on. He replied that this was the first time he came into work for the day and he doesn't wear high heels.

Things that go bump into the night might, just might have a sweet tooth after all.

MATHER-WALLS HOUSE
Keewatin, On.

John Mather (1828-1907) a businessman, known to history as the one who brought industry to the township of Kenora, On. in 1889.

A native of Scotland, Mather travelled to Canada in 1857. Mather became an important person when he acquired the lumber rights to the area around Kenora.

It was then that Mather built The Keewatin Lumbering and Manufacturing Company (KLMC). In its first few years of production the mill almost exclusively produced lumber for the rail road.

Mather hired many skilled and unskilled workers as far away as Scotland. The KLMC was destroyed by fire in 1905.

Three identical houses were built by Mather to house his employees. The second house, built for his son David, is known as the Mather-Walls House (MWH) in Keewatin, On.

In 1893 David moved to Kenora and rented the house to various families including John Walls (1857-1934) and his family. Walls, a native of New Brunswick, was experienced in the lumber trade and in 1883 became a foreman in the Keewatin Lumber Company.

In 1975 the Ontario Heritage Foundation acquired the house. The purpose of the house is to recognize the importance of the Mather family's contribution for the development of Canada.

Jim Doulis is a member of KPS (Kenora Paranormal Society) along with two other members investigates the paranormal in the Kenora area.

Recently, they investigated the MWH.

Variable temperatures are just part of paranormal activity. It was about 15 degrees in the area of the house where they investigated. The temperature jumped to 24 degrees when they investigated the master bedroom.

Three spirits are suspected to haunt the homestead. John Mather, an unknown little girl, a woman in Victoria dress.

People had seen the woman in the window or have felt her presence. She's unusually the one who gives the feeling that she doesn't want people there, explained Doulis.

"It's almost like it's my house, what are you doing?" type of feeling. When people use the Ouija board they also experience that type of feeling. Lots of thumping, unexplainable thumping," said Doulis.

"As soon as we asked a question we would hear the sounds. It was just weird that we would hear the sounds."

"The big one (experience) was the feeling of being touched," reported Doulis.

One of the investigators felt a brush against her arm in the little girl's room.

Liz asked "If there's someone in this room, could you please let us know by either touching Jim or making a sound. That's where she felt movement across her neck."

The room warmed up to 19 degrees from about 11 degrees in the girl's room after what they experienced.

"The little girl wanted us to be there," he remarked.

They also experienced what felt a little like fingers grabbing their wrists.

The KPS says they will investigate more haunting in and around the Kenora area and plan to have a tour for the public this summer about the haunted places they have encountered.

Things that go bump in the night are right down the laneway leading to the unknown.

THE FIVE FISHERMEN RESTAURANT
Halifax, N.S.

There's a building which was built in 1750, located on Argyle Street in the oldest part of Halifax, N.S.

The building was first built as a school in 1817, then Anna Leonowens took the building over as an art school, the Halifax Victorian School of Art. Before coming to Halifax, Anna was the governess to the children of the King of Siam, an experience she would later write a book about called "Anna and the

King of Siam" later movie versions of The King and I.

The building housed the victims of the R.M.S. Titanic and was used as a funeral home for The Halifax Explosion of 1917.

In 1975 The Five Fishermen Restaurant was open for business and it carries non-paying customers which happen to be ghosts. Gary MacDonald, restaurant manager, sent me a document outlining the history of the building.

The document, written by Leonard Currie, stated that glassware would fly off the counters or cutlery would fall to the ground, sink taps would turn on and off by unseen hands. Cold spots, sounds of swinging doors when no one was around are more paranormal experiences.

A waitress saw a gray apparition, a fog-like mass moving down the staircase, near the grand stairwell. Other staff experienced cold spots in heated places, unseen spirits calling out their names.

Another person who was indispensable to this article was Andy Smith owner and operator of Tattle Tours in Halifax. He is well versed in the paranormal of Halifax,

There are two main stories which envelope the restaurant. When the restaurant was closing down a waitress forgot her purse in the changing room upstairs. Seconds, later the staff heard a "horrendous scream," said Smith.

Staff ran upstairs to see if she was OK only to find that she was standing against the wall as if someone was holding her by the neck. "She was looking around for her purse upstairs. When she found her purse she turned around and that's when she found an older man. He took her by the neck and forced her to the wall and then he vanished," he stated.

Recently, one day a medium heard a voice of a young girl coming from the women's washroom area. "He won't let me out; he won't let me out. Mommy come and help me." The medium was challenging the young girl who was being held by the older man.

The older man may have been an undertaker who was stealing from the pockets of the victims of the Halifax Explosion.

The Five Fishermen Restaurant seems to be the ideal place for historians, and tourists or a place where you can have a great meal. Don't be surprised to see something you can't explain.

THE OLD SPAGHETTI FACTORY
Vancouver, B.C.

Things that go bump in the night can be anywhere. They could be in my office, bathroom or even watching me as I type this column or even you reading this.

Vancouver has its share of haunting and those who haunt the

old Gastown area. When investigating Canadian haunts Gastown is a very hotspot.

In 1970 The Old Spaghetti Factory opened to the public both living and dead. Not only does the living enjoy a great meal but the dead or those who are caught between the living and dead also can be seen and felt.

There have been sightings of a male in early 1900s sitting in a trolley car which is situated in the dining room. A man has also been seen in the ladies washroom specifically in the third stall as reported by two separate mediums. This ghost is not a poltergeist (mean spirited) it does seem peaceful in nature. Restaurant employees say the spirit is very active when the dining room is closed.

The spirit enjoys moving the cutlery that is on the trolley. The spirit will even call out the name of the employees which have been employed there for awhile.

Kris Newson was an employee of the Gastown location when he had his own experiences with the paranormal. Newson is now the owner and general manager of the Old Spaghetti Factory in New Westminster location in Vancouver, B.C.

Although he says that he has never seen any spirits he did participate with them. From time to time mediums would visit the restaurant.

One time mediums asked if there was anything they (the spirits) can do to tell Newson that they are here.

"Can you swing a lamp or move some cutlery or move a chair right now to prove that you are here," asked the mediums. "Five seconds later a fork picked up off the table lift around and drop back on the table. A lamp started swinging and chairs collided. This was all visible and audible to us," recalled Newson.

One of the main spirits is Edward who is 11 or 12 years old. "He's the playful one and he's the one who likes to move the cutlery around and unscrews the light bulbs and he gets a kick out of watching us stress about it," noted Newson.

"We converse with about 10 or 12 spirits throughout the day."

There are two main reasons to explain the paranormal activity at the restaurant. One reason is the old train line used to travel under the restaurant in the 1890s. One day there were a massive collision in the tunnel under the restaurant where 92 people perished, said Newson.

Another paranormal reason is a huge church at the end of the block burned to the ground in 1886.

THE KEG MANSION
Toronto, On.

There is a place where they may not always know your name but the name of the place is known by many Torontonians and that of paranormal hunters.

Before we dig into the strange occurrences at The Keg Mansion in Toronto, On. let's see who owned the building. The original title of owner belongs to Lord William McMaster, (1811-1887) who built the mansion in 1867. If the name McMaster sounds familiar, it should. He founded Toronto's McMaster University (later the building moved to Hamilton, On.).

In 1882, at a price tag of $33,000 the mansion was sold to another famous Canadian family by the name of Massey. Hart Massey (1823-1896) founded Massey Ferguson (farm equipment) and Toronto's Massey Hall. He had two famous grandsons, American actor born in Canada Raymond Massey, (1896 –1983) and (Charles) Vincent Massey (1887 – 1967) who was the Governor General of Canada (the first to be born in Canada and served from 1952-1959).

In 1976 the mansion was converted into a Keg restaurant where it now sits. But enough of the history lesson, why does this building make my list of Canadian's Haunting?

Well, one of the paranormal events is that of Lillian Massey (1854-1915). Hart Massey's daughter. Lillian, who died of reasons unknown, at the age of 61, on the second floor in 1915. It's here that people have that "someone is watching me feeling." One day a customer went about their "daily duties" in the bathroom. The locked stall door unlocked and opened by an unseen entity.

One day a customer set her bag on the stall's hook only to witness the bag lift off the hook and set down by her feet.

The upper floor of the restaurant has their shares of weird sightings. For instance, sightings of a boy's ghost have been seen running up and down the staircase and will at times stop and look at the crowd of people dining there. Staff and customers alike have seen ghostly domestic help walking about the mansion. But the famous ghost of all is a maid who hanged herself after hearing the news of Lillian's death. She hanged herself on the second floor oval opening in the main foyer. People have seen the maid with a noose hanging around her neck from time to time.

Since its creation, the mansion has appeared in various TV programs including Alfred Hitchcock Presents and movie Moonstruck (1987) starring Cher. Actors including Telly Savalas, Lindsay Wagner, Lee Majors, Tony Curtis, Tom Selleck, Cheryl Ladd and Kevin Bacon were just some of the rich and famous who visited the mansion.

It's been said many times before that Toronto has all kinds of things that go bump in the night.

HAUNTED FORTS

A person's last request, when it comes to a hanging, is not uncommon. Usually, in today's times, a last request is in the form of a meal. Some last requests were so elaborate that they simply couldn't be carried out.

This is the case of one last request which was not honoured. Fort Henry, Kingston, On., is haunted because the condemned did not have his last request honoured.

A man's spirit is known to haunt a rocking chair. The chair would rock when no one is in it. One visiting family witnessed a man in an uniform while cleaning the uniform. The ghost, named The Wandering Bombardier, is been known to roam the fort. The fort has plenty of hot spots (places where ghosts have been known to roam) as well, nine altogether.

It is known that the bakery is haunted. The Dry Ditch is haunted. To the east of the fort, a spirit called home in Dead Man's Bay, and a handful of soldiers who drowned and now haunt the fort.

Fort George, Niagara-on-the-Lake (NOTL) On. If ever there was a place which is haunted, this place would win hands down. It is been said that NOTL was built on Indian burial grounds.

If a tour is professionally guided, shivers will dance all over you causing you to constantly look over your shoulder into the black darkness for those who bump in the night. I once attended a tour. I was told of the horrors of war and the spirits which roam the fort to this day. It was a tour that I won't soon forget. After some research I found some reports of the haunting which occurs there.

Visitors speak of a grey haired man which observes visitors from behind the bunks in the blockhouses. Another man has been peering out of ground floor windows. A young blonde girl has been seen roaming the grounds wearing a white gown. Another individual has been seen pacing the upper floors of the fort.

Perhaps the most thrilling tale is that of a torso patrolling the gates with his musket at the ready.

Men who were once soldiers fighting and dying in the act of protecting their forts now act as public relations spokespersons to entice new comers into their world they once knew and loved.

They are the few, the proud who bump in a Canadian night.

A SMALL HISTORY OF GHOST HUNTING

Ghost hunting has been around for much longer than most people are aware of. Thanks to the human condition that we thrill to be challenged of being terrified beyond words; and our undying need to know that spirits can communicate with the living the number of people believing in ghosts is reaching ever growing numbers.

The oldest recorded case of ghost hunting is reported by Pliny the Younger in 100 A.D. When he told of the following tale, it was already a century old. The tale tells of a man who bought a house in Athens. The price of the house was far below what it was worth but the sellers wanted to be rid of the house quickly.

The tale says that one night while the new owner was resting comfortably by the fire, a spirit came to him wrapped in chains.

The spirit beckoned him to follow and so he did. He was led to a spot in the garden behind the house where the spirit vanished. The next morning, with the permission of the city magistrates, he dug the spot where the spirit had vanished and found a skeleton wrapped in chains.

Once the body was given a proper burial the haunting ceased.

Ghost hunting followed a renewed interest in spiritualism

caused by two young girls that claimed to speak to a dead peddler. Years later after the claim one girl (now a woman) revealed that the noises heard during the ghosts presents were faked. At the time such a resurgence of interest occurred that no one cared.

The first group that devoted it's time to the search for disembodied souls was a society devoted to ghosts at Cambridge University in 1851. London's Ghost Club started 11 years later. These pioneers provided the beginnings for today's avid ghost hunters.

Enter the mid-1880s William James, a philosopher, suggested applying scientific methods in the search for spirits and ghosts. He found allies in London with Alfred Wallace, Harry Sidwick, Harry's wife Elanor and Edmund Gurney. Together they founded the Society for Psychical Research to collect evidence proving or disproving the existence of ghosts, haunted houses and other paranormal phenomenon.

Ghost hunting would not become a mainstream hobby until the 1970s with the founding of the Chicago area Ghost Trackers Club (which later became the Ghost Research Society in 1981). Today there are over 300 separate ghost hunting organizations throughout America and England and the list is growing.

The three forms of ghost hunting include: the first uses psychic methods to make contacts. Sensitive's (a person who can pick up on spirits very easily) walk through a home and make communication with the ghost or go into a trance. Others may use Ouija boards or other channelling tools to make contact.

The second type of ghost hunter uses something known as "ghost buster" tools. These can consist of infrared cameras, tape recorders and energy measurement tools like the electromagnetic field meter. Pictures of orbs, ectoplasm and spirits represent their proof.

The third type of ghost hunting uses the scientific method. They gather all data and evidence of a haunting and search for normal, natural scientific explanations. If they can find none, then these investigations look to the paranormal for answers.

In my years as a ghost hunter I have photographed orbs but not much else.

Some spirits appear to others that have no interest in ghosts while others, like me, have a strong desire to meet and greet ghosts have a hard time seeing them. One theory on seeing ghosts is that you can see them every day and not even know it.

For instance, if you walk downtown Toronto, you see thousands of people. Are all those thousands of people really from this realm or are some spirits trapped in this world who can't continue to the next?

THE OUIJA BOARD

You might say the Ouija board is not a Canadian invention and you would be right. But most readers know about or had some experiences with an Ouija board. Some say it's a parlour trick while others swear that demons use them as portals from hell to the living. Whatever your take on the subject, it has a history and here it is.

The Ouija board (from the French and German words for *yes, oui* and *ja*, pronounced also known as a spirit board or talking board, is a flat board marked with letters, numbers and other symbols, supposedly used to communicate with spirits.

It uses a planchette (a small heart-shaped piece of wood) or movable indicator to indicate the spirit's message by spelling the message out on the board during a séance. The fingers of the séance participants are placed on the planchette, which then moves about the board to spell out messages.

Ouija is a trade mark for a talking board currently sold by Parker Brothers and can be purchased in Canadian stores such as Toys R Us.

Following its commercial introduction by businessman Elijah Bond in the late 1890s, the Ouija board was regarded as a harmless parlour game unrelated to the occult until American Spiritualist Pearl Curran popularized its use as a divining tool during World War 1.

Mainstream Christian religions and some occultists have associated use of the Ouija board with the threat of demonic possession. Some have cautioned their followers not to use Ouija boards. While Ouija believers feel the paranormal or supernatural is responsible for Ouija's action, it may be more explainable by unconscious movements of those controlling the pointer, a phenomenon known as the ideomotor effect. Despite being debunked by the efforts of the scientific community, Ouija remains popular among many young people.

One of the first mentions of the automatic writing method used in the Ouija board is found in China around 1100 B.C., and it is first recorded in historical documents of the Song Dynasty.

The use of planchette writing as a means of ostensibly contacting the dead and the spirit-world continued and albeit under special rituals and supervisions, was a central practice of the Quanzhen School, until it was forbidden by the Qing Dynasty. Several entire scriptures of the Daozang are supposedly works of automatic planchette writing. Similar methods of mediumistic spirit writing have been widely practiced in Ancient India, Greece, Rome and medieval Europe.

During the 1800s, planchettes were widely sold as a novelty. The businessmen Elijah Bond and Charles Kennard had the idea to patent a planchette sold with a board on which the alphabet was printed. The patentees filed on May 28, 1890 for patent protection and thus had invented the first Ouija board. Issue date on the patent was February 10, 1891. They received U.S. Patent 446,054. Bond was an attorney and was an inventor of other objects in addition to this device.

An employee of Kennard and William Fuld took over the talking board production and in 1901, he started production of his own boards under the name *Ouija*. Kennard claimed he learned the name Ouija from using the board and that it was an ancient Egyptian word meaning *good luck*.

When Fuld took over production of the boards, he popularized the more widely accepted etymology that the name came from a combination of the French and German words for yes. The Fuld name would become synonymous with the *Ouija* board, as

Fuld reinvented its history, claiming that he himself had invented it.

The strange talk about the boards from Fuld's competitors flooded the market and all these boards enjoyed a heyday from the 1920s through the 1960s. Fuld sued many companies over the Ouija name and concept right up until his death in 1927. In 1966, Fuld's estate sold the entire business to Parker Brothers, who continues to hold all trademarks and patients. About 10 brands of talking boards are sold today under various names.

I have an Ouija board. I even used them in my investigations of haunted houses. I keep the board in my storage unit and not in my house, because you just never know. If Ouija boards do bump in the night, they can do all the bumping they want to outside and not in my home.

THE IRVING HOUSE

There are many homes which are haunted. When they are being

first built, they are called buildings, then they can turn into a house and when a family moves into them they become homes.

If a famous person resides in these homes they can become museums only if the right people look after them. If these museums stand the passing of time and enough strong events take place there, they can in fact become haunted. The Irving House in Victoria, B.C., is a haunted building where peaceful spirits still occupy the home.

William Irving was born in 1816 in Annan, Dumfriesshire, Scotland. In 1859, William Irving and his family moved to Victoria where he became a partner in the Victoria Steam Navigation Company and built two sternwheelers. The Governor Douglas and the Colonel Moody, to serve between New Westminister and Victoria.

However, Irving did not have a monopoly on the route and rate wars soon erupted between him and his main rival, Captain William Moore who was running his Henrietta on the same route.

By that September, freight rates, which had begun at $12 a ton, dropped to 50 cents a ton and fares, which had been $10 a passenger also dropped to 50 cents.

According to the Irving House website the house was built in 1865 for Captain William Irving who was an important figure in the river trading industry of the Lower Fraser River in the late 1800s. The house was built in the Carpenter Gothic Revival style of architecture and has some features reminiscent of architecture from Irving's homeland, Scotland.

Archie Miller, owner of A Sense of History Research Services Inc. in British Columbia was the curator and lived in the basement suite for 26 years. In his residency there he came across some paranormal activity.

A dog he had responded to noises in the middle of the night with a low growl. He could sense that Miller was scared. Since the home is a public place he thought people were walking by looking into the house. It was in the main hallway where sounds of people pacing came from.

"I thought I got people on the property," noted Miller.

I could definitely hear people above my head. I know sounds of the house and the sounds the house makes, he stated.

"I can hear this pacing. I started to go up and confront them (people) and the sounds stopped. That was one (incident) that was quite profound. The captain himself died in the house. We think a couple other people died in the house. If you're looking for a candidate (spirit) probably the best one is Captain William Irving."

Irving's son John was close to the house but didn't die in the house.

That still could make John a candidate for a spirit that haunts the home.

The sounds of rustling skirts were heard over the years. One incident over the many years include the following: A visitor came into the house when she was greeted by a tour guide. The visitor noticed another woman behind the guide dressed in costume of the Victorian time. The person in custom turned and vanished into the wall.

A woman who was sensitive to spirits said that the house was so full of spirits that she had to step outside to catch her breath and never came back, noted Miller.

Another incident of yesteryear included when a child, who was sickly, visited the caretakers long ago. When the child went to John's room she saw a man lying in the bed and reported it. There was a major indentation on the bed when the others came to see the mysterious man.

The Irving House definitely has some pretty weird events going on there and the spirits bump in a Canadian night.

MYLAR & LORETA'S RESTAURANT
Singhampton, On.

Mylar & Loreta's restaurant was built in the 1850s and comes with at least three visitors from the other side. According to its website, Cyrus Sing was the first owner and probably built the hotel. It is not known if Mr. Sing operated the hotel and had many locals working for him.

In 1863, the hotel was sold to Robert Hannah of Stayner for $60. It changed hands again in 1870 and the new owners changed the name to The Blackstock Hotel. Mrs. Blackstock purchased the hotel from her husband, Edward, in 1887. Thomas Brown was the owner and rented rooms as a hotel.

In 1914 Mrs. Blackstock bought back the hotel and rented it to John

English until 1919, when it was sold to Hugh McKenney for $900. During the 1920s the hotel was a popular spot for Toronto people who would come for the weekends to fish. These weekend people were the ones who filled the hotels allowing the owners to make a living.

From 1928 to 1973, the hotel was operated as a general store with various owners with living quarters above. It was converted to a restaurant in 1973 and operated as The Hampton House until 1983. When the present owners took over. operating as Mylar & Loreta's.

Who is or was Mylar and Loreta? Read the following poem found on their website to find out.

T'was 100 years ago or so that Mylar left his home. To find his fame and fortune, in the new land he would roam.

His journey was a long one, but finally he found. A home here in Singhampton. with good friends all around.

He talked of a fair lady, the finest in the land. Loreta's heart was bursting, her stately ship set sail.

The sky was bright, the sea was calm, no thought of stormy gale.

Then came that night of terror when her ship went down at sea.

Her soul released to heaven, her spirit was set free.

Some say she came to Mylar's, it's difficult to know.

His love for her kept growing. He could never let her go.

Now as you sit and dine today and enjoy our country inn,
Feel the power of their special love that lingers from within.

Sandy Hamilton has been the owner of the building for over 20 years. She said that customers have seen items "fly off the shelves as if someone gave them a push from behind."

Hamilton has her own experiences at the restaurant.

"Mylar has a few places where he likes to be and by the kitchen door is one of them. He just stands there.

I'll realize someone is standing there as I look up towards his space to see who it is; he disappears right in front of my face. He wears dark pants, suspenders, a red plaid shirt," she said. "As soon as you try to focus on his face he goes away," she continued. "He has literally opened drawers.

"One customer will never come back after witnessing a paranormal event where a drawer opened and no one was there to open it," explained Hamilton.

Hamilton's father has heard voices like people were fighting downstairs when no one was there. The hauntings have been ongoing even before she became the owner. One of her customers has seen a man, lady and child by the fireplace. One customer said that the lady ghost looks like she's prim and proper but she's not.

Perhaps she is a mischievous spirit or a woman acting unbecoming of her times. Another customer has seen a lady ghost when the customer visits the washroom.

Mylar & Loreta's Restaurant is home to ghost roaming near the fireplace or by the kitchen doors. They seem friendly as they bump in a Canadian night.

CAMBRIDGE PARANORMAL INVESTIGATORS

Glen Murphy is a member of the Cambridge Paranormal Investigators which is based in Cambridge, On.

Since 2009, they have been investigating paranormal places, some with and without success.

Murphy says by watching shows like Paranormal State and Ghost Hunters sparked an interest in the paranormal field.

"I always had interests in that sort of stuff."

Dreams of past relatives also had an influence on producing a paranormal group.

"I'd like to do something like that," he stated.

So, off he went and purchased some spirit detecting equipment. An EMF (Electromagnetic Field) reader is a tool which can detect either magnetic, electric or both types of field together. Ghost hunters use this type of equipment but he is not 100 per cent positive that they work for finding spirits.

"With EMF I'm not 100 per cent sure of those things because they pick up electricity and other stuff."

In the winter, static electricity is a major concern when tracking the paranormal and EMF readers will often pick up static giving a false reading which the tracker thinks it is a spirit.

Murphy will give advice for those about to hunt for the paranormal.

"You really have to have a knack for it. You have to have nerve as well. I've been in some pretty creepy places. I usually don't get creeped out."

At present, Murphy's group are five strong but people come and go all the time.

"They join the group and something happens and they leave."

Murphy knows the importance of a hobby.

"You have to have the will for it. We don't do it (investigations) all the time, we do it when we can. It's not our job. It's a hobby but we do take it seriously."

Once a neighbour's house had a spirit which the group managed to get rid of that was on the border of splitting the family up.

The old post office (formally Fiddler's Green Irish Pub) in Cambridge is haunted. When the group investigated the attic they later played back the audio and heard voices when no one was there.

"It was definitely interesting. It was pretty cool."

While investigating the pub, a friend told Murphy to point the camera in a corner of the kitchen and when he did, something unusual happened.

"So when I pointed my camera up there, my infrared light went out on me and when I moved away, it went back on. When I checked the batteries, the batteries were fine."

We would like to get back in there (pub) but our calls go unanswered, informed Murphy.

"I believe the place is creeped out for sure."

Time of day really doesn't matter when paranormal hunting is concerned.

"Paranormal activity happens all the time. We investigated a house out in Woolwich (township). We've been there three times. The first few times we were there, we got lots of activity even though it was very subtle. The first time we were there, we got someone breathing on audio, a voice of a little girl saying *momma* and a man's voice saying *here they come*, referring to us in the back of the building.

"The second time we were there, I heard a woman's voice in the attic. I asked *are you happy here?*

"When I played the tape back, I heard, *no I'm not happy here.*

"The third time, recently, we didn't get any feeling of the paranormal. The owners were moving out, so the house was quiet. We usually get feelings right away. Maybe the paranormal activity left with them. The owners of the old house say that there are things going on in the new house."

Things that go bump in the night may be hard to detect, but with the right equipment they may not be hard at all.

THE GHOST WITH NO NAME

This story originally took place in the fall of 1908, winter 1909.

The place of this particular event was at a sawmill owned by William Cockerill at Crerar Lake (or as locals know it as Dark Lake) in the northwest Ontario.

The sawmill employed workers and they lived at the mill year round.

One day, a man came to the sawmill and wanted directions to the forest reserve. The man was in trouble by the nearby Grandview police. The man had all the appearances of a classic hobo.

A pair of pants was hanged around his neck and it appeared that the legs were stuffed with unknown items and he had a classic hobo stick with a red hanky which was also stuffed with something.

Not long after that, the men at the sawmill, started hearing knocking in the walls of the cabin.

According to the article An Old Family Story written by Barbara Smith (published in Ghost Stories of Manitoba) the knocking was not confined to any particular place. It was heard on the ceiling, walls, floor, and even in the middle of a frozen rain barrel.

One particular cook's aide hated the ghost. She would be standing in the middle of the kitchen and all of a sudden she would have a great big chunk of hair pulled right out of her head. A big bruise appeared on her arm where she was pinched by the ghost.

The sawmill workers who witnessed the sounds thought the person responsible to the knockings were that of the ghost of the mysterious stranger who asked directions awhile ago.

Communication was attempted to speak to the ghost by a series of knocking. The men would ask the ghost questions and the ghost would communicate to them. Two knocks for no and three knocks for yes.

Billy Angus stopped by the mill one day and was welcomed to stay the night. After dinner that night Angus was told of the ghost.

According to the book, shortly afterwards, a quilt started to move about on the bed like a mink or something was under it trying to get out. When they lifted the quilt, there was nothing there.

A board similar to an Ouija board was used to finally communicate with the ghost.

According to the story, the ghost spelled out to them that he had been killed by a bear over by a certain tree near the mill.

After further investigations, the bones of a human foot and leg was found at the sight the ghost said they were to be found. The identity of the ghost was never known.

THE WALTERDALE PLAYHOUSE Edmonton Alta.

Theatres and playhouses seem to be a magnet to visitors from the beyond. The Walterdale Playhouse is no stranger to the strange and the paranormal. Since the building is over 100 years old, it is certainly prime for those that bump in the night.

The playhouse was founded in 1959 by the Walterdale Theatre Associates, and it is one of Western Canada's oldest amateur theatre groups. Since 1974 Walterdale Theatre Associates has been located in the heart of Old Strathcona in the oldest fire hall in Alberta. Strathcona Firehall No. 1 (later Edmonton No. 6), which the associates converted into the Walterdale Playhouse.

Built in 1909, the firehall is now designed a Provincial Registered Historical Resource. This venue seats 145. In 1994 the theatre received an award for Outstanding Contribution to the Performing Arts. To those in the Edmonton community it is a meaningful part of the arts and theatre culture enjoyed within the city.

With the exception of a paid part-time administrator, the playhouse is operated entirely by volunteers with a love of theatre. Members of any age and background have the unique opportunity to participate in all aspects of live theatre.

Richard Hatfield, Technical Director, emailed the following experiences he had with the playhouse.

Usually when it comes to research I enjoy talking to the witnesses of the paranormal face to face or on the phone. But since time is extremely valuable, email will do in a pinch. Here, in Hatfield's own voice, are his experiences with the unknown.

"As a tech at the Walterdale, I have had the need to be in the building late with few or no other members of the team with me. While teching a few shows over the years, I was in the building alone quite late. I knew there was no one else in the building, but heard footsteps upstairs. I immediately went upstairs to check, but all the lights were off and no one was in sight.

"A more recent unexplained situation was during our last show *The Best Little Whorehouse in Texas* that I was stage managing. One night, I heard an excessive amount of moderate to heavy walking upstairs. Since that type of walking could be heard by the audience, I immediately announced over the speaker to upstairs "Please, walk quiet upstairs!" All of the cast upstairs looked at each other oddly apparently and came up to me at intermission to say , "Everyone was seated for a while before you asked us to be quiet. There was no one walking around at all."

"My entire booth crew heard the walking, so I know it was not in my head. Needless to say there was a moment of "ok, well. that's odd..." As to not alarm anyone who may have issues with the unexplained, I basically excused it to that cast as

"Maybe it was front of the house that I heard."

"Of course there is no way it could have been then since they are on the main floor that is concrete and below where I am seated, not above. All in all, I have heard some unexplained foot fall (and it is definitely an unmistakable foot fall/walking sound), but other than that, I have had no other experiences with our ghost. Quite frankly, I do not feel uncomfortable at all. If anything, the extra sounds that occur due to our friend from beyond when I am at the theatre after hours is somehow comforting."

THE CUSTOM HOUSE
Hamilton, On.

Old houses and buildings seem to have a life of their own.

They have been seen and felt numerous events through their existence. At times unfortunate incidences such as a death may have occurred within their walls.

The victims, of tragic events, may have all but been forgotten but their spirits linger on.

Travel now to Hamilton, On., where the building, formally known as the Custom House, has seen its share of things that go bump in the night.

The Custom House, sits at 51 Stuart St., was built in 1860. Its function was to house the customs department. In its 149 years the house have been a home to an army recruiting centre, a flophouse (cheap boarding-house), a martial arts academy and even a macaroni factory.

The Ontario Workers Arts and Heritage Centre (OWAHC) reside in this haunted building.

The first document sighting, of a female spirit, came in 1873 by Alexander Wingfield, an employee of the Custom House.

Now, no one is sure who the lady of the house was but throughout the ages she has been coined the Black Lady (BL) or Dark Lady (DL).

Fast forward to 1940 where three female students of Murray Street School; located behind the Custom House witnessed and event that would have emotional consequences.

What they said they saw was a slightly transparent figure of a beautiful woman in the top floor of the house. Their experience was so traumatic that 37 years later when they retold their experiences they were still frightened of the figure.

Is the BK/DL alone in her haunting? A certain woman had her own experience with a male voice telling her to "get out of here."

Unexplained breezes, doors opening by unseen hands and

electrical equipment have been reportly operated when no one was there to operate them.

In 1996 major renovations consumed the OWAHC. When the workers ended a hard day of work they returned to a fresh day only to find tools scattered over the house.

This would not be a big event if the workers had not put away their tools the night before. Once the workers found their tools stacked (called stacking in paranormal terms) up in a pile.

Jim MacDonald, a painter, was told by a spirit that, if during the renovations a certain mantelpiece was removed, the result would end in a flood. Perhaps not at biblical proportions but a messy costly flood nevertheless.

Low and behold, the item was moved, a flood ensued resulting when a roof drain broke.

The flood was the straw that broke the camel's back for many staff members. The staff suddenly believed in spirits that haunted the building.

But the strange events didn't stop here. Not by a long shot. A volunteer of the OWAHC, James Newbauer, was on his first night. Nothing was out of the ordinary when he shut windows and locked the fastening bars on the shutters. But only seconds later, when Andrew DeNew, a fellow volunteer and Newbauer found them unlocked.

I was once a visitor of this majestic building. A few years ago during my visit I too felt a chill at the main staircase and my digital camera picked up orbs (a mass of spiritual energy).

I visited many supposedly haunted buildings and places but a few places have compared to the Custom House. I had the feeling of being watched. Perhaps not by a lady but someone or something knew I was there.

Manufactured by Amazon.ca
Bolton, ON